The syllables that remain
        Are echos
Crashing down the sky
    in handfuls of dull glitter
        Everyone I've loved

        is gone

Alas, dreams
—
Those hidden dens

Dark Ansley

02

A pioneering publishing house dedicated to creating intelligent, vivid books. Established to inform, educate, entertain and provoke.

A Backlash Press Book

Published 2015, 2024

backlashpress.com

ISBN: 978-1-0686972-1-0.

Dark Ansley
02

Gret Heffernan

And many of those who sleep in the dust of the earth shall awake, some
to everlasting life, and some to shame and everlasting contempt.

Daniel 12:2

To Mike, Eddy, and Ayla.

1

The birds pecked Jude's eyes and wedged their beaks between his scales like little hammering syringes. The flock was massive and looped and dived like a single animal as it lifted the serpent and carried him out to sea, beyond the blue blaze of Hastings. Marianne took Dex's hand, held Emoli with her other arm, and together they watched Jude writhe through the fire-lit sky.

Their escape from the snake didn't seem real.

All around them hummed the acute sense of living that a close brush with death delivers, as though their very cells were titillating inside the air, sweet and poignant with spared life. All they could think about was how they'd been saved, rescued by the birds, when moments before they'd felt the black panic of the end. And, now, suddenly there was life and it seemed at once both fragile and indestructible.

Jude was gone.

The pearl was safe inside of Emoli, whose skin was shining like a lantern.

The new world was ready to activate.

***

Martin stood camouflaged by shadows at the edge of the woodland. She watched the castle and the surrounding rubble for signs of movement, a cherub or a survivor, and only when she was sure they were alone did she sound her birdcall. Dex recognized it straight away and responded with a birdcall of his own.

"What was that?" Marianne held Emoli protectively to her chest.

"An old friend," Dex said. "She's the one who saved us. Come on," and he ran in the direction of the call.

Martin watched them running across the uncontaminated field. Dear God, she thought, the infant was already glowing. The seed was more powerful than she had imagined and the urgency to begin the preparations overtook her sensibilities. She turned and lifted her hands towards the beech tree, as if offering a service. The pearl's lake had soaked into the ground and all that remained was the tree, unattached and levitating, with roots as large and exposed as its branches, it leaned towards her outstretched palms.

Martin began to sing, a low drone that impelled the tree to creak and twist, slowly, at first, as though stretching after deep sleep. Martins voice became louder, fiercer, and when she thrust her hands up towards the sky, the tree began to rapidly grow. She chanted as her palms pulsed the tree upwards, so by the time Marianne, Emoli, and Dex reached the woodland, long coils of bark twisted into the sky like brown and gray hydras, and the tree had nearly quadrupled in size. It scared Marianne.

"What's happening?!" Marianne shouted above the tree's gnarling, she clutched Emoli who was too stunned to cry.

"Martin!" Dex called, and Martin visibly tore herself away from her incantation and joined them.

"Dex," Martin took his hands, exhausted but vibrant. "I've set the activation in motion," she said, her arms were outstretched towards Marianne. "Welcome," she hugged her and Emoli as one.

Her embrace was intense and Marianne could feel the power inside Martin effervescing, while behind them the tree continued to grow. Martin released Marianne, held her by the shoulders and looked penetratingly into her eyes.

"We have waited so long for…" an arrow narrowly missed Marianne's ear.

Martin pushed Marianne and Emoli to the ground and covered them with her body. "Bloody cherubs!"

2

Two cherubs were flying across the field, loading arrows and shooting at them. Branches, gnashing like teeth, intervened and flicked the cherubs' arrows away with ease. Martin grabbed Dex's arm.

"Do you remember the way from here?" she asked, and Dex nodded yes.

"Good. Go then. I won't be long," she said.

She shifted into an enormous condor, sailed towards the cherubs, dodging their arrows with ease and picked up each one with a single foot. Their chubby flesh ballooned from inside of her talons as she flapped in the direction of the sea. Within seconds, Martin had dropped their small bodies into the blue fire of Hastings.

"Let's go!" Dex shouted over his shoulder.

They ran through the woodland and reached the cliff tops of the South Downs. Wind bent the grass and spat rain against their faces. Marianne kept looking back at the brewing storm above the treetops, the beech tree's branches looked as though they were streaks of lighting that pierced the clouds with slashes of silver. The sky was all the colors of a bruise and flashing.

There was no time to think, to register what was happening. They could only concentrate on one foot in front of the other and safety. It was like stepping from one life and into another already in motion. She had to believe in Dex. He was all she had now.

Where was he taking her?

At last they reached the used car lot. It looked empty, but when Dex made a birdcall, the rusty door of an old Buick opened. Dex ducked inside and turned towards Marianne. His eyes were bright as searchlights. He held out his hand.

"Trust me," he said.

The world was on fire.

What else could she do?

They crawled across the car seats to where earthen steps led down into a room that had been carved out of the hillside. A woman in the corner ran her fingertips along the walls of packed soil, and where her fingers touched, light glowed. She began drawing a picture with the light. Two figures and a small child with a glowing ring around them. Inside the child's chest was a star, and from it other stars began to spawn, some formed animals that leapt, swam, and flew between the lights.

The picture lit the room. Marianne could see small white roots dangling from the ceiling. The woman stopped drawing and, breathless from her exertion, approached Marianne. She was younger than Martin, but wore the same boiler suit, had bronzed passionate eyes, and wild bird's nest hair. She looked at Emoli and placed the palm of her hand upon his forehead.

Marianne began to pull him away, but Dex stopped her. "It's okay. She's reading him."

The woman hummed the same low hum that Martin had used to grow the beech tree. She began to flicker like a hologram and with each flash the transparent image of the pearl surrounding her grew stronger and stronger. When she broke away, she staggered backwards, and thrust her hands towards the ceiling. The lit stars lifted from the walls and circled around Marianne, Dex, and Emoli like a thousand fireflies.

"The seed of Genesis," the woman said, her face, voice was full of rapture.

She bowed.

Martin opened the car door and stepped down the stairs. The woman lifted and exchanged a nod with Martin, and then both bellowed an ear-splitting screech. In moments, a rumble of wings blanketed over them, bits of soil dropped to the floor, and it sounded like a large animal had landed on the cars above them.

"What was that?" Marianne asked, it was the first time she'd spoken since the tree and her voice sounded alien to her.

"The birds have obscured us from any wandering cherubs. Head under wing and in thousands they resemble a hill. You and the seed are welcome and safe here," said Martin, as she stepped closer to Marianne and placed her palm on Marianne's forehead.

"Ah, you have moth wings instead of a bird's. I knew you were winged," she said.

Unnerved, Marianne flinched her head away from Martin, "I can become a moth, but I can't control them or anything," she said.

"What do you know of your powers?" Martin asked, and the wings seared across Marianne's back began to burn.

Martin's voice was soft and maternal, Marianne felt herself both reassured and intimidated by her words. It was true. What did she know of her powers? What did she know about herself at all? Martin seemed to be reading her mind and smiled knowingly.

"It will all become clear," she said, and turned her attention to Dex.

"Well done," she said, and hugged him. "You fought valiantly and survived. And what of your other friend? The colorless one?"

"You mean Ansley?" Marianne interrupted. "You know him? Dex, why didn't you tell me?"

3

Emoli, trying to catch the floating stars, rocked back and forth inside of Marianne's arms. The woman remained unmoving in the corner, as though she was meditating, and Marianne and Martin stared at Dex waiting for an answer.

"When?" Dex asked. "Between finding your parents, hiding the seed and battling a murderous snake, exactly *when* did I have the time to tell you?"

"Fine," said Marianne. "There is no need to be defensive and I don't want to argue about it now, but for the record, it matters to me. Ansley matters," she took the ring from her pocket and gave it to Martin. "This is all we have of him."

"You think he's dead?" Martin looked at both of them. "Strange, I didn't feel him pass."

"We know he's dead," said Dex, and he put his arm around Marianne's shoulders.

Martin noticed Dex was holding his breath and accurately sensed that there was something they weren't telling her. "But, then, I have been focused on the seed," she said, and looked directly at Dex. "The seed is what is important now," and Dex nodded. "I am sorry for your loss, but I suggest you keep that ring somewhere safe," she told Marianne. "The dead can still surprise the living. Now come and I will show you inside. You must eat and rest."

She reached into the front pocket of her boiler suit, pulled out a brown feather, and blew on it. The shaft lit like an illuminated baton, which she stuck in the back of her thick hair and motioned for them to follow. The tunnel they entered was hollowed out of the earth and large enough to stand up inside. It was fortressed by row after row of semicircular arches of metal like the steel ribcage of a whale. Martin ran her fingers along the walls and each arch, one by one, as though setting a ripple in motion, lit and beamed neon green.

Ahead of them a wall of car doors fused into focus and Marianne could see that they were slotted together like a finished metal puzzle that blocked the end of the tunnel. Martin stepped forward and lifted the handle of a small rusted door, causing the whole wall to open and release a metallic glow.

"The heart of us," she said, and stepped to the side, so that Marianne and Dex could enter.

The opening was cathedral sized and reinforced with an egg-shaped brace of crisscrossed steel. The enormous room smelt and looked burnished. In the center was a fixed and gigantic Ferris wheel with skeletal car frames painted in bright colors hanging along its spokes and around its rim. The cars had been completely stripped, sofas or pillows replaced the seats, and curtains hung from the old door and window frames. Small wood burners glowed inside some of the dwellings and the people navigated along interconnecting ladders bolted to the Ferris wheel.

"Welcome to our community," Martin said, and whistled softly.

Above the Ferris wheel hung a magnificent scrap-metal sculpture of a pair of wings, and a few welders, hoisted by a crane, were busy working on it. A small bird flew through their sparks and landed on Martin's arm.

"Your guide will take you to your rooms. Join us for a feast when you are ready. Until then, rest. We are so pleased you are here," she said, and walked away leaving them alone for the first time since Jude's attack.

"How do you know these people?" Marianne was awestruck. "Are they shifters? Or witches? Or mechanics? Or what?"

"Martin is a shifter and a witch. Though I am not sure about her following. She was one of Wakehurst's first seed collectors and a friend of my parents," Dex said.

"Wait a minute, first seed collector – how old is she?" Marianne asked.

"A shifter's human body does not age when they are in animal form. She spent many years moving from one animal and into another," he said, and held his hand out to the bird.

"Right. That doesn't sound entirely stable to me. Are you sure we can trust her?"

"She has given everything to save the seeds," he said, and the bird landed on his arm.

"You say that like she lost something," Marianne said, as she shifted Emoli's sleeping weight.

"She did. She lost her partner, which is why she couldn't stand to be human."

They followed the small bird to their room, a gutted Land Rover on the Ferris wheel, fitted with a foam mattress and plenty of bedding. The wood-burning stove had been lit in preparation for their arrival. The three lay down together and listened to the sound of welding. Orange flashes behind the pulled curtain ignited the purple vines stitched across the fabric. Emoli smacked his tiny gums in his sleep and Marianne watched him. His glow was iridescent and his skin was almost completely transparent, she could see his veins and arteries as though he were marbled.

"How will we hide him when he's like that?" Dex asked as he propped himself up on one elbow.

"Maybe we won't need to. Maybe we can just wait until he expels the pearl and we can plant it again," said Marianne, as she stroked Emoli's little snoring nose.

Dex ran his finger along Marianne's shoulder and lifted her chin to look at him. "I'm sorry I didn't tell you about Ansley. It wasn't intentional, it's just, so many other things were happening, you know?"

"I know. I just. I'll miss him," she said, and laid down next to Emoli. "I loved him."

"So did I," Dex said, and he thought, but not as much as I love you.

***

Their tiny guide flapped gently against their faces to wake them. Marianne sat up and looked out of the window. Everyone was gone and the space was silent, but for a slight industrial drone. Emoli began to whimper.

"He's hungry," said Marianne, as she picked him up and patted his back.

"Do you know where to get some food?" Dex asked the little bird, and with that, the bird hopped down the metal staircase affixed to the Ferris wheel and onto the steering wheel of an awaiting bumper car.

"I guess this is our ride," said Dex, as he opened the car door for Marianne and Emoli.

Between the seats was a small bassinette and Marianne fastened Emoli into place before she put on her own seatbelt. The car jerked to a start and sparked along a metal track hanging from the ceiling like exposed pipework. Now that the Ferris wheel was empty a flock of martins fastened the ladders to the undersides of the carriage cars and the whole wheel began to slowly rotate. The metal bird at the top rose and fell and Marianne saw that its wings were bellows. The car drove around the back of the Ferris wheel where they could see the bellows blow air down a flue attached into a garage sized brick furnace. The air was suffocating and they could hear the fire snapping to life with the bellows blow.

"Now we know how they harness their electricity," said Dex, as they drove past.

"This whole place is like a dream," said Marianne.

The spokes of the Ferris wheel rotating above her like the cogs of some bizarre clock producing a low and deep mechanical hum-like resonance. All of this had been happening beneath her feet, she thought, under her nose and awareness, and she thought of how this could have been a world for Ansley. There are places for everyone, she thought, it was just a question of locating the where you belong. She wondered where in the world she would fit? Perhaps that is why the idea of a new planet had been so desirable; perhaps there was no place for her on earth.

Emoli glowed like a moon beside her and they entered a dark tunnel, again ribbed by neon metal archway and Marianne felt, once more, as if they were entering the oesophagus of a whale. Marianne put her hand on Dex's shoulder and turned to face him, her hopeful face blinked on and off as they moved under the green arches.

"Do you believe there is a chance that Ansley's still alive?"

4

Did he? Dex asked himself. Did he believe his friend was dead, or, perversely, was that just what he wanted to believe?

Emoli squealed between them, whatever the case, there was no time to find Ansley and Martin was right, the seed was the most important thing. But, also, he had to admit, there was a part of him that just wanted Marianne to himself. He had been so lonely. He had lost everyone. Was his desire to hang onto her something he needed to feel guilty about? No, he decided, and took her hand.

"I think he's dead," he said, and she nodded.

It wasn't complete lie. An emotional death and a physical death were parallel events in this world. He would be dead soon enough, thought Dex, if he isn't already. He mourned his friend and thanked his luck.

Ahead, they could hear the faint sounds of music and murmured speech as though listening through a stomach. The bumper car suddenly dropped down an old shaft and stopped short before two large metal wings. The wings parted and the room was full, hot, and alive with martins.

The room resembled a burrow with a large nest in its center. Woven into the nest were hundreds of chairs with armrests containing bowl-shaped indentions. The martin women sat in these chairs talking, and playing music or cards. The ceiling was domed and looked as though it too were woven with branches, feathers, bracken, and scavenged cloth.

The drawn stars from earlier danced in and out of the ceiling's hiding places. Emoli cooed and waved his hands to try and catch them. A few dipped down and playfully teased him as they spun around his head. When Marianne looked closer she realized that they weren't stars at all.

"Dex! Look inside their shine! There are numbers and letters – this one is an eye!"

The eye floated in front of Dex, as though it had heard Marianne, and blinked.

Martin stood and opened her arms wide. "Come and join us!" she shouted across the room, and the music and conversation stopped.

Bowls and instruments were put down and the women rose and began to clap. Emoli followed suite and the applause became a joyous uproar. All of the women wore the same boiler suit and had wild, often dreadlocked, tangled brown hair. Inside their hair they carried bones, twigs, and feathers. The sound of their applause reminded Marianne of flapping birds.

"You bring us so much happiness," said Martin as she approached.

She lead them to two chairs and a highchair woven into the center of the nest. A woman approached with bowls of steaming soup.

"Sit and eat," said Martin, then she raised her hand and the applause immediately stopped.

Marianne put the radiant Emoli into the highchair and a woman arrived with a spoon to feed him. As he ate the stars spelled his name and trailed their lights like lettered sparklers. He squealed delightedly between bites and rocked his chubby body back and forth to the music. Drums, guitars, and ukuleles mixed with the chatting voices of the women, while Dex and Marianne drank their soup. It was a vegetable broth with a hint of cardamom seed.

"Thank you," said Marianne. "I didn't realize how hungry I was."

They both placed their empty bowls into the armrests, and when Martin raised her hand a woman appeared from a small chamber that had been dug into the side of the room. Inside this chamber was a long and flat cooker that had been bolted together with scrap metal. Inside the cooker roared a fire that heated a huge skillet, and on top of the skillet a cauldron of soup boiled steadily. The woman ladled more soup into their empty bowls.

"We don't have much," Martin explained. "Most of what we get we take to the camps for the survivors."

Dex and Marianne felt guilty for their greed.

"You are welcome to what we have," Martin said. "Don't worry," she smiled. "You need it for the journey and we have enough to spare."

"Are you a mind reader?" Marianne asked, as she drank down her delicious broth.

"No, more of a feelings reader. You get to know animal nature, including human nature, very well when you have been around as long as I have," said Martin.

"Why aren't there any survivors here?" Marianne asked.

Dex was busy playing with Emoli, catching stars, and spelling things, they were all in happy moods now that their stomachs were full. He leaned in to listen to Martins answer.

"Well, in the simplest terms, it's not their flock. We can only house those with the power of wings, but perhaps that will change. Who knows? We have set the initiation in motion and, to be honest, we aren't exactly sure how it will unfold. How a path manifests is only half related to where it started, the other half is down to intention, trust, and chance. These are the things I know: Marianne holds the power of wings and will be given her instructions soon. The Growers are already in place."

"The Growers? Who are the Growers?" Dex asked.

"The Growers are the ones that hold the seeds inside them," said Martin.

Their guide flew down and landed on Martin's shoulder, she cocked her head to listen to the small bird, then rose with alarm and released one of her ear-splitting screeches.

"What's happened?!" Marianne shouted as she took Emoli from the highchair.

"Cherubs!" Martin grabbed Marianne's arm. "Quickly!"

They ran to the winged door and when they reached the tunnel, a dozen birds were hovering with their backpacks and a quilt from the bed. Martin reached up and took the quilt.

"Wrap the child in this so his glow isn't visible," she said.

Marianne did as she was told while Dex grabbed their backpacks and they followed Martin to the entrance of another tunnel.

"The cherubs have attacked," she said, lit her feather and stuck it in her hair to show them the way.

"But I thought nobody could see through the winged fortress," said Marianne running alongside Martin.

"They can't," Martin replied. "That's the point. Somebody must have told them. Somebody from the inside," she turned to Dex as they reached a spiral staircase, kissed his cheeks, and held him. "I wish I had more time," she whispered. "Listen, much has changed within the seed-collecting world. Remember your mother's instinct Dex," she turned to Marianne and took her hand. "You will receive your instructions soon. Be ready for them. Be ready for anything. Now, follow the stairs to the top and you will reach a trapdoor on the ceiling. Push it open. Inside is a safe house. The next time I see you, I will address you by your mother's favorite game," she said to Dex. "Otherwise answer to no one claiming to be me. I must fight now," she said, and touched his cheek. "Be safe," she extinguished her light, shifted into a vulture, and flew through the tunnel in blackness.

"Come on," Marianne said, as she tied Emoli to her chest with the blanket. "He's awake. Let's go before he starts to cry."

They felt their way up the stairs to the ceiling. The trapdoor was barely visible and covered in dirt. It took both of them to push it open and Dex hoisted Marianne and the infant through the other side.

"What can you see?" Dex asked, squinting so the dirt wouldn't fall into his eyes.

"You're not going to believe this," said Marianne. "It's a bridal shop."

5

Although it was embarrassing, it was good to cast off that loathsome idiot Simorg and return to his pure snaky skin. Good riddance, he thought, I'll never again inhabit a microbiologist, far too methodological, and he pushed Simorg to the bottom of his dark mind. Jude's lair lay trapped in a water pocket beneath the earth's surface like a boiling cauldron of swamp water. When its rock walls shifted it created the creaking pops of an upset stomach and he found this very comforting. It was once completely dark, but years of humans pissing all those pharmaceutical drugs into the leaky drains of sewage treatment plants had created glowing pharmacurrents of green toxicity. The pharmacurrents carried illuminated fish mutants in and out of the earth's polluted bowels, above which the cherubs were busy chiseling shelves along the cavern walls to house Jude's collection of DNA. It was a spectacle of great beauty and Jude had dreamed it into existence, even so, even amid his hollow of toxic splendor, he was not satisfied and felt downright melancholy. His sigh was long and pathetic.

The birds' attack had left him damaged. Those winged terrors had taken him out into the middle of the ocean and dropped him, beak punctured and bruised, into the water. He sank to the bottom of the seabed, an unloved coil, then painfully slinked though a hydrothermal vent and into his lair to recoup. It was a catastrophe. Their talons had ripped and damaged many of his scales and he was an old snake, so couldn't immediately shed his skin again. It was the waiting that crippled him, however, it also gave him time to devise a plan. And a plan was definitely needed, as it would be impossible to simply eat the child, for the pearl's radiance would definitely kill him. He would have to steal Emoli, but how with all those birds flapping about? And was it possible to muddy the little brat's waters in order to eat him and be done with it? It made his reptilian brain ache. Still. There were things to be grateful for, the scale was in place, and there was nowhere that they could hide. And his lair, he fondly looked around, his beautiful lair, like a nesting place for dark thoughts, as though every-thing sinister had been absorbed into one big ball and lovingly squeezed. Being here always gave him medicinal drops of perspective, yes, something would rise from the murky depths of his genius, like it always did.

He bathed and did laps in his swamp's waters while the cherubs finished unpacking his jars of DNA. It was pure physio bliss. Then he entered his bedroom and coiled beneath his beloved chandelier. It was good to be home, he thought, as he closed his eyes and slept.

His lair was a stilted antebellum house built above the cavern's noxious waters. He had dismantled from an abandoned plantation home in Florida that he'd fallen in love with while on holiday. It wasn't as palatial as most antebellum homes, but the woodwork was elegantly detailed and the house itself had the poise of faded glory. The cherubs painstakingly took it apart and placed each piece inside a massive storage container along with bundle after bundle of Spanish moss.

Jude pushed the container through an enormous hydrothermal vent, punted it down the toxic river and into his cavern, where the stilts had already been prepared. It took a year for the cherubs to put the house back together. Inside the library he stored the jars containing his favorite souls. The Michelin-starred chef, the ballerina, the man who made amazing balloon animals, a couple of poets, and a bass guitarist, to name a few. His planet wouldn't be without culture, mind you, even a snake has dreams.

The only difference Jude made to the original house design was the construction of a crow's nest on the pitched roof, where he loved to curl and ponder to the lapping florescent water. When the house was finished he strung Spanish moss from the rock walls and wooden rafters like hanging tinsel on a Christmas tree and then began his decorating pilfer in earnest. It's amazing what you can move in a storage container when it's properly packed, of course, this feat of steel perfection allowed him to push his beloved baby grand piano through a hydrothermal vent. A fact that left him eternally appreciative, for the cherubs only had their little mini harps and flutes that sounded like howling alley cats. One particularly annoying cherub played the piano, and really, it was the only reason Jude hadn't eaten him. When Jude woke up he fancied some music.

"Bring the pianist!" he shouted from his crow's nest.

Large spiders crawled down from the cavern walls and began to web over his wounds. The cherubs tended to appear and multiply like monkeys and hundreds of them were floating inside the cavern now. Bows, quivers, and arrows attached to their chubby chests.

"Go away!" He hissed at the ones flying above him. "How dare you hover above me with underdeveloped bladders!"

And *this* is my army, he despaired, but put on a brave face anyway.

The pianist took his position on the bench and started to play. Jude rolled his yellow eyes.

"Do you *seriously* think I want to hear the Messiah?! Who do you think I am?! Jazz, you idiot, play jazz!"

He let the spiders' nursing and the music clear his thoughts. When they had finished dressing his wounds he felt renewed and warm as though he were tucked inside a large sock. He would have to attack, he decided, no more lazing about. The seed would only grow stronger in the girl's presence. He needed to take the child now and worry about extracting the seed later. Who knows? Maybe nature would take care of that for him? Although he doubted it would be that easy, nothing ever is, he thought, as he rose to full height and addressed the other cherubs.

"Now, I know I might look like an overgrown sock puppet, but, listen up! The birds' attack would have killed a lesser snake," he began. "But I've used it to my advantage and have taken the time to reflect and plan. I'll give you the coordinates of Marianne and I want you to attack en masse and relentlessly. My radar tells me that she is underground.

Shoot until you find the opening. I will instruct the heliflies to leave their positions and help you. Now go! And find that child!"

***

The cherubs flew swiftly up and out of the hydrothermal vents, while Jude slunk back down among the comforting clicking of the spiders. Their legs moved deliberately under his dressings as they continued to clean and mend his scales. He thought about Emoli.

How to turn Emoli's water? He needed him close enough to influence, yet not close enough to burn him. He needed him to be submerged in his sentiment.

Below him a little spider was toiling away. This is what he loved about the insect world, they just kept silently altering the planet without anybody noticing until the shape had taken place. There is much to be said for toiling away under unsuspecting noses. And this spider wasn't just any eight-legged gypsy, oh no, she was a water barer. A mutant water barer with a built-in reed. Meaning she lived under water for protection, but couldn't breathe there, so made a bubble of air with a snorkel attached to a reed. Genius. Proof that you can work your way out of anything, especially if you are a mutant, he thought, and that's when inspiration struck.

Jude had the spider make two bubbles, one for himself and one for Emoli, so the two of them could float together like wobbly bosoms. It was where he'd store the little rug rat until he was infected enough to eat. Figuring it out was like being born again. He spent all afternoon in his bubble and felt entirely recuperated.

Above him he could see the floaty faces of the cherubs looking down in distress. He hissed at them. They jumped back and the water lens made their flesh wiggle more than usual. Their faces showed real concern. They were speaking to him and motioning for him to rise to the surface. He poked his head out of the bubble's snorkel.

"This had better be good," he said.

"We've attacked the used car lot master," he said.

"And? How many did you manage to kill?"

"A few," the cherub said. "The rest shifted into birds and flew away."

"Damn those shape-shifters! What about the child?! Tell me you haven't lost the child," Jude's eyes narrowed.

"No, of course not. A helifly followed the scent of the girl and the baby is with her," said a cherub, and the others nodded in agreement. "They'll are sleeping," he said, "unguarded."

"Unguarded?" Jude laughed. "A whole world and they left it unguarded?! They don't deserve a planet. Hurry up. We mustn't waste another minute. Don't just stand there! Fetch me my 'going out' fedora," he said, slinking out of his bubble and using his tail to position the hat firmly on his head.

"But master," said the cherub, "do you think you're well enough to make the journey?"

"What choice do I have," he said. "As if I'd leave this job to you," he looked at his swampy reflection and tilted the hat a little to the left. "It's showtime."

***

The abandoned wedding dress shop was perfect and surreal. In the back was a huge storeroom and in the middle of the floor were at least fifty mannequins wearing wedding dresses.

"It's like a ballroom," Marianne said, as she crawled out of the trapdoor.

Dex followed her. "Yeah, a ghost's ballroom."

Dex picked up a veil and draped it over a mannequin's head and started turning her head around and around as though she were possessed. The place was creepy, but hidden and warm.

"Which one would you wear?" Dex asked.

"I'm not the marrying type actually," said Marianne.

"Really? So, what are you then? The type that just has illegitimate children with random genetic freaks?" Dex spun the head of another mannequin.

"Stop it, you're scaring him," she said, altogether avoiding the conversation.

"No I'm not. Look at him. He had that face when I shifted into a wolf, bemused awe, and by the way, little daddy becoming a wolf is not exactly a great role model either," Dex said, and spun another head to make his point.

"You're not his daddy," said Marianne.

"And you're not his mother," said Dex.

"I never said I was," Marianne rubbed her temples. "We're his guardians," she sighed and changed the subject. "Do you think Martin will be okay?"

"I've never known her not to be," he said, and lifted a large silk ball gown. "This thing is big enough to sleep under."

They went to the hanging rack and collected half a dozen silk dresses for bedding, then crawled inside the tulle bell. Fatigue had robbed them of the ability to think of anything else. It was like being inside a tent. It was cozy and almost soundless. Marianne wrapped Emoli inside the blanket and he fell instantly asleep.

"Excellent. It's like a tent with knickers," Dex said as he curled up next to Emoli.

"Goodnight Dex," said Marianne.

The helifly had waited until each of them had fallen asleep before he flew to the cherubs and gave them the tip-off. An hour later, the dresses fluttered like nervous brides as Jude slid soundlessly under each one until he found Emoli. Ding dong, he smiled, opened his mouth wide, and carried him gently away.

***

Two years later.

6

Beatrice's protector popped out his eyeball, forced it into the lens of a small retractable telescope, and handed it to her. Compressed, the telescope was the size of a thumb. Beatrice put the brass thumb in her pocket. She knew this was going to happen. For weeks now she had been prepared for her Grower initiation to take place, but knowing her story didn't make it any easier and she trembled with anxiety.

She knelt beside his bed and held his hand. The skin stretching over his knuckles felt like cold parchment paper. He hadn't the strength to clear his throat and his breath was caught on a gurgle. All at once his body arched like a wooden bow then sprang flat. His mouth was opened round. It reminded her of that screaming painting. His remaining eye was as large as an egg and she had to stop herself from turning away.

"Shhh. Don't struggle," she told him, "I'll be fine. I know what to do. You've trained me for this. I'll see you soon," she said.

She placed her hand on his wet forehead. It was like touching a damp stone. Very slowly his eyelids closed, soon his breath was like a clock that wound to a stop, and his body took the stance of a discarded glove, as if he'd vanished.

She hugged herself and watched the fire snap the black curtain of her shadow against the wall. He was dead and there was no one else.

There was no guarantee that they'd come for her. Only her protector had kept her safe and fed during the final purge. Yet sometimes she wondered if he'd only told her the story of the Growers to give her an identity to believe in, a reason to continue.

Her tears fell fast and plentiful. At first the water soaked into her skin as if she were a made of plaster. The water, the water felt so glorious on her face that she cried all the more for her excess, for her waste.

And then it happened.

It sounded as if a bead had dropped on the floor, then ten beads, one hundred beads, as if a necklace had broken against the stone floor. It seemed as if her tears were scattering. When she cupped her hands around her eyes, and brought them down again, they were full of seeds. Tears came rushing out of her and each one became a seed.

She was crying tiny black seeds.

So the prophecy was true and her initiation had begun.

She looked at the seeds on the floor, bent down, picked one up, and squeezed it between her thumb and forefinger. It indented her skin. It was real enough. She got down on her hands and knees and scoured the floor for seeds. Seeds! She thought, real seeds! She had been prepared for her Grower initiation, had imagined it a million times, but this? This was astonishing. She filled a drinking glass and placed it on the table. She stood pressing her finger into the glass of seeds like indenting dough. Truly astonishing.

The last three seeds lay beside the hearth like shiny black bugs. She was just about to collect them, when the fire curled like a snake's tongue and licked them up.

Had that really happened? She watched them burning on the fire, burning green, small wisps like billowing grasses.

Were those faces? She leaned forward. The fire was so enticing. Her eyes were mirrored balls the fire danced inside as if its flames were the wind's red dresses, were sirens, beckoning, summoning come, come. She was reaching towards its heat when suddenly there was a knock at the door.

She pulled her hand back and stood. The fire hissed and slunk back into its iron basket like a sly animal.

She wasn't expecting a Grower so soon. It was well past midnight and she had assumed they would wait until morning. She was afraid, because she knew as soon as she opened the door, her life would change forever. But wasn't that the point? Hadn't she only been hiding, coaching for the moment to start living? Even a life in limbo has a certain comfort to it and change is always difficult. Another knock, not loud, but solid and intending. There is no escaping fate, she thought, so she might as well step up to it.

"Yes?" she called out as she walked towards the door.

"It's Oren," a voice spoke. "First Grower activated."

She unlatched the lock and opened the door. In walked a tall figure in a black hooded coat.

"Boy it's cold out there," he said blowing his hot breath into his hands.

He put his hood down, uncovering eyes as gold as coins, and bowed his head in the direction of her protector. He saw the seeds in the glass on the table. His eyes widened like two bright suns. His hair, brown as a mushroom, curled softly from his head.

"Beatrice," he said. "I'm so glad I found you," he stepped forward and held out his hand for her to shake. "It's nice to meet you at last, you know, put a name with a face."

She shook his hand and nodded. "It's nice to meet you as well," she feigned a politeness she did not feel.

She wanted to shout, punch, and scream.

"I'm sorry about your protector," he glanced in his direction. "I loved mine as well. But you'll see them again, of course they'll be different, but then everything's different now." He looked around the room suspiciously. "Are you alone?"

"Yes," she said, the question caught her off guard.

"Who made the fire?" he asked, pointing his finger towards the hearth.

"I did," she answered.

He filled his cheeks with air and blew across the room extinguishing the fire. The room fell completely dark. The seeds inside the glass released a glowing green mist that curled up to the ceiling. In the haze she saw the green seeds reflecting in his eyes like emeralds on two golden plates. He reached into his pocket and pulled out a blue iridescent ball that he threw in the direction of the hearth. Out of its core a fire instantly sprang.

"From now on, don't trust a fire made without a charm," he told her.

"Is that why it came to life?"

"What did? The fire?"

"Yes, just before you arrived. It snaked out of the basket and ate three seeds," she said, feeling naive that she didn't know about the charm.

Everything was already new and different.

"It was the fire sprites. They can possess any flame. What they do is lure you in and smoke out your soul. A charred soul is like flint to them. It gives them spark," he said.

"I see. Do they work for Jude?"

"No, you might say they're evil freelancers," Oren laughed and rubbed his hands next to the fire. "We are susceptible to the supernatural now, being magical ourselves. Crazy isn't it?" He looked at her cup of seeds on the table. "Did you cry yours as well?"

"I can't believe it, but I did," she sat on her knees in front of the hearth and added some wood.

"I know, it's mad," he knelt down beside her and put his hand on her shoulder. "It took me a day or two to adjust as well. Come on," he said, standing. "I want to show you something," and he helped her to her feet. "Follow me and bring your telescope. You're going to love this."

They walked out into the cold night and she clutched her sweater to her throat. He pointed to the roof of the house, everything was silent and black, until she put her telescope up to her eye. Through it she saw a ribbon of green smoke curling beyond the clouds as thin as pulled apart gauze. Her locating signal.

"That's beautiful," she said.

It was why they collected their seeds as soon as they were shed, so the mist, like a veil, could rise and the signal could release.

"It's our call to one another," he said. "I followed it to you. Amazing isn't it? Now look at me," he said.

She brought the telescope back up to her eye and saw that a haze of yellow fog surrounded Oren.

"Your light. I can see your light," she said. She could hardly believe the telescope actually worked.

"What color is it?"

"Yellow. What about mine? Can you see mine?"

Oren took his telescope out of his pocket, brought it up to his eye and looked at Beatrice.

"Blue Beatrice," he said, and smiled.

"Blue. I like that. I like the idea of being cloaked in blue. Have you seen anyone without light?"

"No, and fingers crossed we won't," he said, and looked at the end of his telescope. "Do you think it's really their eye?"

"Of course it is. I saw my protector take his eyeball out and stick it in there," she turned her telescope around and her protector's dark leopard eye looked up at her.

If it had an eyelid it would have winked.

"Seriously? Mine didn't do that. He even pulled a patch out so I wouldn't have to see a gaping hole," he said, still looking at his golden eagle eye.

"That sounds very considerate," she said.

"You mean formal," he said. "He was very formal. It was a job, you know? He rarely shifted out of eagle form. I couldn't wait to be activated, I couldn't believe it when it happened and now it still feels like a fairy tale or something."

"Yeah, I know, like someone else's story and then suddenly," she said, and put her palms up into the air to indicate "this."

"And then, suddenly, it's yours and you're in the middle of living it," he finished for her, and she hummed in agreement.

Beatrice looked through her telescope once more, as if willing her initiation real. Her eyes followed the green smoke twisting like a beanstalk though the clear black sky and beyond, the stars so bright they were winking like hidden, conspiring, animals.

"It's cold," Oren broke the silence and rubbed his arms.

Beatrice opened the door. The fire, ablaze and orange, radiated its heat against their faces as they stepped inside. Her protector's pale and silent body glowed in the firelight like a mountain in the setting sun. Beatrice walked towards him and ran her finger down the slope of his nose.

"Let's take care of him," she said affectionately. "It's time he was given his heart."

7

A small pouch dangling from a silver chain was attached to her studded belt. She unlocked it and held it up for Oren to see. They straightened their backs and prepared for the coming ritual.

"This is the skin of a leopard and it needs its leopards heart," she nodded towards her protector.

Oren nodded as well and she opened the pouch. An enormous black leopard sprang out and landed on the lifeless chest of her protector. It began tenderly licking his face. Oren moved closer to Beatrice and placed his hand on her shoulder. She looked at him.

"There are no words for it," he said. "Just watch."

She looked back at the leopard and gasped. Her protector's skin had begun to dissolve like sugar under the leopard's hot tongue. In a few moments there was nothing left of his body save a small, red, beating heart. The leopard held the heart lovingly in his black paws before swallowing it whole. He then turned his majestic head and looked straight at Beatrice. It was almost as if the leopard had smiled. She whistled, here boy, opened the pouch, and the leopard jumped inside and disappeared. She placed the pouch on the table. The glass of seeds deepened their green glow.

She poured the seeds into the pouch and they, too, disappeared. The pouch felt warm and soft in her hands. She rubbed it over her cheeks. She put her nose inside its soft fur and breathed it in deeply. It smelt of fresh air and meat, just like her protector.

"Now you're free with all the others," she whispered.

"Waiting for us," said Oren.

The space where her protector's body had been filled with a peaceful firelight.

"Yes," she whispered. "Waiting for us."

***

What Beatrice remembers of her first life, the life she had before she became a Grower, is vague. She recalls Marianne curing and saving her. She recalls the boat, a sucking sound, and her soul hovering above her like green wisp, when the boat suddenly rocked and before she knew what was happening, she was dangling from her protector's mouth. He was in leopard form and had her by the scruff of the neck.

Her first vivid memory began with the green blur of ferns and trees racing behind her floppy legs. She felt his warm spit and panting breath against her skin. Even then, she felt safe.

He took her to a burning city. There was an abandoned confectionary shop front with red and white curtains. There were jars of rock candy sticks in the window and when they opened the door a little bell chimed. She remembers how absurd the bell sounded among the smoke and blue fire. Her protector walked behind the countertop and took down a jar of sweets as though he knew what he was looking for.

He had shifted into a human, but unlike any human she had ever seen, his body was formless, sexless, a eunuch, and covered in a fine black pelt. Only his face, hands, and feet were covered with the skin of a man. He reached into a jar of butterscotch sticks and pulled out her telescope. Its brass body had been perfectly camouflaged inside the toffee-colored sweets.

"There is no time to spare. I'll explain later," he said, as he shifted into a leopard again and grabbed her once more by the neck.

He leapt out the door and a second later the shop exploded. She remembers there was fire and running. Everything, everyone was running, bleeding, and blurring. She was a small girl dangling from a leopard's mouth in a sea of frantic legs. Buildings blew up all around her and black burning rocks spat out of the fire like demented birds. People kept trying to grab her. They thought the leopard was taking her away, stealing her as food or something.

He saw a big metal garbage can and jumped inside it. It fell over sideways and they began to roll down the hill, too fast for humans. The metal became hot to the touch. With every bounce the side of her arm was thrown against the edge of the metal. She had to stop herself from screaming. She watched the sweetshop burn. It was a red flaming ball that spun around and around and when she closed her eyes she saw it still, for ages, she saw it spinning.

At the end of the street the hill steepened. She remembers the smell of burnt grass. At the bottom of the hill was a drop off. They crouched down together and fell into the sea. Only her hair whipped and whirled out of the metal opening, splash, the water was hot and streamed into her open mouth. He grabbed her around the waist and pulled her to the shore. She coughed, spat, and sucked in the air.

Everything was eerily still inside the inlet, the water was metallic in color and lapped as a solid thing, a tongue. They hid behind the rocks and out of the cliffs she fabricated jagged faces, pitted noses, shadowed eyes. He said there would be no survivors that they could trust.

They would have to travel now, he said, and he would tell her who she was. He found a crab and cooked it. He told her she was a Grower. That she had been reborn. She agreed because she was hungry. He handed her one of the rock candy sticks. It was pink and yellow. It was her first sweet, she sucked it and stared out to sea while he tended the crab. If she weren't so amazed by all of the things that had just happened, she would have been devastated, but that came later.

***

The life of a Grower is a strange one. You know your story. You know your purpose is to carry the seeds to the new world but you do not know how you'll get there. You do not know the path you'll take. Her protector had told her that while fate is decided, the path is a gift. Sometimes it's wanted and sometimes it isn't.

Mostly, it wasn't the path she would have wanted. Mostly she was hungry and tired and lonely. And as the days passed the new world took on the fantastical sheen of a childhood dream. When faced with the realities of survival, it seemed as far away and as hidden as her hope of ever finding it. The truth was that she had thought of the new world less and less. Of course her protector told her the stories, but they had become sleepy bedtime incantations and she found her mind meandering like a stream. Her thoughts and his advice, his stories swirled together and like sieving water, there was no real way to capture or separate the two. Now that it was here and happening, she was scared.

"Are you okay?" Oren said.

"I've only ever half believed," she said, adding another log to the fire. "It's just starting to sink in I guess."

Outside the wind snapped and threw sand against the walls. She felt foolish and immature. Wasn't he apprehensive? Did he feel capable of igniting a new world? She watched him beside the fire. His long fingers perched over his knees like talons. His lashes like black feathers with cheekbones as jutted as branches. He really did look like a bird.

"It just takes a while. Personally, I can't wait for the scattering. I dream of who I'll become on the new planet. I remember my life before you see. I remember my family's contamination. My parents, my little sister," he shook the thoughts from his head. "So many times I've wanted to explode those visions from my head," he said.

She nodded. Soon he would get the chance to scatter.

"You should be getting your tattoo about now," he changed the subject and lifted his shirt. "Look at mine," he said.

Snow-capped mountains sprang from a black circle around his belly button like a ring of splintered teeth. The face of an eagle shimmered like a hologram inside the circle then vanished. Every Grower received a tattoo after their initiation. It was like an umbilical connection to their protector, without it they wouldn't be able to harness their protector's powers.

"What was it like having an eagle as your protector?"

"It was great," Oren said. "You wouldn't want to be afraid of heights though. Or the cold. We lived in the mountains," a look of longing came over his face. "The air was so thin it felt as though it could lift you off the ground. Sometimes I believed I was flying."

"That sounds magical," she said. "Were there others?" Beatrice pictured him perched on a cliff edge with his arms spread, his nose hooked.

"My protector called it a colony, but I rarely saw the others. They nested above us and searched for higher mountains where the snow never melted. I circled the thermals with them and they communicated with loud shrieks. Often the others brought me food though, squirrel, jackrabbit, all skinned and ready for the fire. My protector said it was because I was their final hope," he lifted his shirt once more and traced the mountains with his finger.

They glistened with his touch as though they were glass against firelight.

"I can't tell you how often I think about that," he said. "Me, a boy from Bromley giving an eagle hope," he shook his head in awe. "Bloody miracle."

She smiled. "Have you seen him since stimulation?"

"No. But I haven't needed him. They only come when they're needed. I do miss him though," he said.

"Is it true your rebirth involved an egg?"

"It's true, but I don't remember very much about it. Only that it was really warm and soft," he said. "My seeds were inside the egg."

"How did you get out? I always expected you to have a clawed thumb or a beak or something," she said and smiled.

"Well you haven't seen my toes," he winked.

"Are you serious?"

"Completely," he said.

"Well, come on, let me see them!"

"Maybe on our second date. I have to woo you with my personality before I show you my gnarly bits," he said, and laughed.

"Really. I assumed your personality was your gnarly bit," she said.

He started to reply but yawned instead.

"Am I boring you?"

"Not at all. Sorry. I'm just so tired," he said, and yawned again.

"I know. Me too."

Beatrice rose, took two blankets from the bed, and handed one to Oren. For a moment she stared at the place where her protector's body used to be and gently brushed the indention with her fingertips. She took the pouch and the blanket and lay down on the floor. She was exhausted. Outside crows squabbled under an austere sky. The sun was beginning to rise, like a harsh red lash across an open eye. It was hard to believe that only five years ago there had actually been grass. The virus had killed almost everything.

Beatrice could hear small funnels of sand grind against the walls. There were no windows as windows eroded too quickly in this landscape. They had been here for nearly a month subsisting off of dried meat and little water. What would she have done if Oren hadn't come? She hates to admit it, but sometimes she'd wondered if she was merely saved by a crazy wizard and the story of the Growers was just something he made up. It was real, she thought, there was another world. She pinched herself. It was real and happening.

She closed her eyes and listened. She wished Oren would to talk to her. She wanted his voice to enter her mind and slide the scrambled pictures behind her eyelids into place. Perhaps he could bring some sense to it all? But he was silent. He balled his coat up like a pillow and placed it next to the dying fire. He laid down on it and stared at the ceiling with his hands clasped on his chest. Blades of sun sliced the room into fragments and inside them rivers of filament swirled. A prism of sunlight cut across his face like a scar. He didn't move. He took a deep breath and fell asleep. She followed.

She woke in the late afternoon heat. A small bracelet-sized circle outlined her belly button. She traced her finger around it like drawing a circle in the sand. She could feel her old self blowing away. Her skin was as taunt as an apricot and the same shade. The circle was a moon with smudgy black clouds on either side of it. She saw her leopard's eyes twinkling like conscious stars. She realized he must have been in the sky when they were watching the green smoke. Oren woke up and watched her inspect her stomach.

"They should be coming for us soon," he said. "They'll take us to the beech tree, but first we need to go to London to pick up some guy named Dark Ansley."

8

"London?!" Beatrice asked, alarmed. "Why?" She did not want to go to London as London was full of outcasts.

"Marianne said we couldn't fulfill our duty without him. He has a special condition that keeps him out of the sun, so he's all ghostly white and, well, we need him because he's the only one in the world that can pick this special fruit from the phosforest."

"The phosforest? Are you serious? That's like sending someone to a guillotine," she shivered. "Once we sheltered in a cabin near the phosforest's edge and you could hear the cries of the bloodpigs and the vines chewing at night. It was terrifying."

"I know. I've watched it growing from the air. It's so tangled, it's like one creature blocking whole sections of the sky and redirecting clouds. To avoid it we would have to fly so high that we would feel as though our lungs were going to collapse," he said, and thought of Dark Ansley. "Poor sod."

"What's it all about?"

"I don't know. Marianne said she'd explain it in detail when we got back. She and Dex want to speak to us all together. I'm just following orders," he said.

Marianne and Dex. Beatrice could hardly believe she was speaking about them in the present tense. She could hardly believe the Collectors were real people.

"So, you've met them. Wow."

"Only briefly. You've met them too you know."

"But I was too young to really remember it. Too young or too shocked. Anyway, it was a lifetime ago," she said.

That time seemed to play itself back like an old film and she felt nervous to meet Dex and Marianne. Mostly she and her protector had just been hiding and she didn't know what was in store for her initiation.

"You know why we were initiated don't you?"

"Not exactly, but I'm assuming Emoli has been found?"

"I thought that too, but Jude still has him," said Oren.

"Jude? How will we rescue him in time to initiate?"

"I'm guessing that's what Dark Ansley is for. Otherwise they'd never risk us going to London," he said. "Look. I hate to change the subject, but I'm starving," he said as his hand disappeared into his stomach and pulled out an apple. He bit into it. "Your seeds should be embedded now. Give it a try," he said, smirking.

Her hand seemed to absorb into her stomach.

Immediately it touched moist soil. It was incredible. It was as if she could see with her fingers. She moved her hand along the soil until she felt a sticky vine that she recognized as a tomato plant. Her fingers crawled like caterpillars up the stem until she felt the juice-filled skin of a tomato. She picked it and gently pulled it out of her navel. It didn't hurt at all. She watched her stomach smooth like a rippled pool that stops wobbling. She placed the tomato on the table and sat down beside it.

"I didn't think it would happen so quickly," she said.

"One of the perks," he finished his apple. "How long has it been since you've had a tomato?"

"Years," she said, and looked at her hands.

Small grains of soil were stuck to them and she licked them clean. They tasted of a distant memory. In her mind she saw tomato plants growing against a wall of pale stone. She could smell them. She watched a butterfly dip between their fat hairy leaves. A baby sticks her fingers inside the rich earth, supple as fur. The baby eats the earth. Two hands reach towards her and a face masked by the bright sun as if it were the sun, outlines a deep laugh of golden light.

"I think I'm remembering my mother," her eyes fill with tears. She washes her face with her hands rubbing the smell of tomato vines all over her.

"What is happening to me?"

"It's all growing inside of us, everything is growing inside us, continuously, we're like walking gardens, rainforests, woodlands. We host the new world now." he said.

"I know that. I don't mean physically, I mean emotionally. I haven't felt anything in years and now I'm a blubbering idiot," she wiped her nose.

"You're not a blubbering idiot. I don't know. Maybe it's just because you have new life inside you."

"Yes. A life that's awakened."

She shook her head as if to shake the memory off and takes her knife out of her pocket. She cut a thin slice of tomato and put it in her mouth, letting its juice slide down her chin. She caught a running drip with her finger and sucked it.

"Oh my God," she said, and her head swirled back with rapture.

"Taste-bud heaven huh?" Oren said.

She snapped her head up again and quickly swallowed.

"Did you hear that?" she asked.

"What? Just the wind I expect."

"No, I know all the sounds the wind can make in this place, believe me. There's a tapping at the door. Hear it? Should I open it?"

"Cautiously, very cautiously," he warned.

She opened the door with her knife in her hand and saw nothing. She looked around. The sun set was on the horizon, its pink rays like tender scars across the flat sand. A little sandstorm emerged from the distance, like a tiny tornado moving closer and closer, only there was something alive and animated about it.

"What on earth is that?"

Oren came up behind her and laughed.

"That would be our ride," he said, and before she had time to question him, a sailboat composed entirely of moths docked before them, waiting.

Oren stepped inside and held out his hand.

"I can't just leave," she felt incredulous. "I need to grab a few things."

"Look," he said, and pointed.

Sure enough, moths shaped like hands were loading up her books and few belongings. They placed them gently into the rocking boat. Then the moth hands lifted her arms and legs and gently placed her into the boat. Suddenly she remembered the telescope her protector had given her. She touched her pocket, it was still there.

They sailed level with the orange setting sun. The moths' wings caught and aimed the evening's crimson light into a moving design like swirling crystals. Traveling through the sky in bowl of cut glass. Their tiny antenna and hairs glistened and rolled as though the air were water.

Beneath them, Beatrice could see the petrified remains of burnt timber spiking through the sand like a serpent's spine. There is little else. A few crows. The scared irregular scrambling of lizards and rabbits. The phosforest in the distance like a menacing mouth.

She looked up. They were unimaginably close to the stars. She imagined swallowing one and lighting up. She imagined her veins glowing red-blue and sinewy as though she were a leaf held against a flashlight. She felt warm, liquidated, her skin was a glass that held her swishing inside. She had long since forgotten the water inside her. The wind whipped a piece of hair into her mouth. It tasted sandy, salty, and human. It had been so long since she'd felt the thrill of wind, of water, of anything.

She and her protector had traveled mostly by night, sneaking out in the cool dry darkness, avoiding the moon and lit fires beneath it. Avoiding life, she thought. You must survive, her protector repeatedly told her. You must hide until the time is right, he had said. And now she felt so exposed, exposed, yet safe inside this fluttering womb, as if her chest were a chrysalis that had cracked open and the reason for her survival was crawling out of herself. It is bigger than her, alien, and majestic destiny. She began to comprehend her importance. She looked down at her stomach, all the components of life are within me, she thought, of course that had always been true, but now it rings out to her like a celebration. Why hadn't she noticed it before?

* * *

Below them, London writhed in the distance like a huge struggling animal. A place, a thing, can either look beautiful or terrifying in firelight. Beatrice couldn't decide which, perhaps both. Space and rubble surrounded most of the buildings like brick and concrete avalanches at the base of still gray mountains. Inside the buildings the eyes of burnt-out windows smoked and flickered. The river Thames had long since dried. As they flew over it the crows and pigeons flapped up, uncovering a collection of silvered bones all locking together like a twisted alien spine snaking through the middle of the city. The occasional discarded refrigerator poked out like a calcium cyst.

"Modern art," said Oren.

Beatrice had to laugh. There was actually something grotesquely attractive about it. The moths took them to Hampstead Heath and lowered the boat so they could step out.

"Looks like we're walking from here," said Oren.

"Do you know the way?"

No, but I'm guessing he does," Oren said, pointing to a single moth fluttering just ahead of them. It seemed to be waiting.

They looked at one another.

"Here goes," said Beatrice, and they began walking towards the city.

9

After Jude had destroyed the castle, Ansley walked straight down the center of the M25. The occasional stopped car was rusted and burnt out like a relic from another world. The sky was at its violet hour and the clouds were a thick crust of red. The only sounds were his feet on the pavement and the intermittent bird. It wasn't difficult to believe that he was the last person alive. The almost empty motorway led him into the middle of London, like an arrow, and only stopped when he saw the lions outside the National Gallery. The pigeons were fluttering around their cement manes and roosting on their eyelids and hind legs.

Can we ever guess what will give us pause?

Ansley sat down on the wide steps and watched. The night air clung to him like a gray moss and the city filled his pores. There was no traffic or electricity, but there were a few people. They crossed empty streets or emerged from deserted buildings, walking like shadows that had been wound from the back and released. A couple of windows were broken, a few doors were missing, but otherwise the city seemed relatively intact, however desolate.

When value in object is taken away, what is there to steal?

A woman peeked around a traffic light, ran towards him, and dropped to her knees about ten feet in front of him. She was kneeling beside a small dandelion poking through a crack in the pavement. Its stem was green, which meant it wasn't contaminated, plus it had gone to seed. Without taking her eyes off him, she dug her fingers into the crack and pulled out the weed, roots and all, without setting drift a single dandelion clock. She carefully stored the seeds in a plastic bag and popped the rest of the plant greedily into her mouth, then vanished behind the lions.

He stared in her direction for a long time.

A few fires shook inside greasy windows and up against building walls.

What would become of him?

More and more pigeons arrived until there were hundreds of them, cooing and flapping their frayed feathers. Finally he took out his notebook, rubbed his hand over its slightly charred cover, and wrote:

The syllables that remain
are echoes
crashing down the sky
in handfuls
of dull glitter.
Everyone I've loved
Is gone.

He could feel the loss of his father, Marianne, and Dex cracking through him like an earthquake releasing a steam of pain that he could barely breathe inside. He put his head in his hands and sobbed. The pigeons surrounded him, one carried an old discarded piece of wax paper in its mouth, the kind a food vendor uses, and released it in a panic of wings. Ansley peeled the paper from the step it was blown against and took a pen from his pocket. He used the side of the pen to iron out the creases and dried his eyes. He stared at the paper for a long time before deciding what to write. Nothing seemed adequate. He wrote the names of those that he had loved and rolled it up as thin as a drinking straw. A few of the pigeons were pecking the grime around his shoes. One had an old tracking ring attached to its foot. Very carefully Ansley slid the paper through the ring and when it was secure he stood up and clapped his hands. The pigeon took off and Ansley watched it fly into the darkness carrying his message. It was the only ritual he could think to perform and he hoped it was enough. When the bird had vanished, he laid his head down on the cold cement step and slept as though he, too, were dead.

⁣⁣*

Months later, when he remembered the pigeons, he wondered how he ever let so much food go to waste. Of course time had begun to lessen the sting of then, but it hadn't rubbed out the pain and his memory could plague him. He had tried his best to forget. He had tried to become a machine. When he thought of himself he tried to imagine gears, nuts, and bolts inside his chest. He imagined his veins were wires and his arteries steel pipes that his blood, a molten metal, traversed through. Metal. He wanted to be metal, that's all, then rust.

10

Ansley was calm during those first few weeks in London in the same way that the devout are calm in a disaster. Perhaps it came from the time he'd spent in the dark, anyway a certain quietude had inhabited his center, like the inside of a monastery. The pearl had sent a speck of dirt to float down his single shaft of light and settle on the floor that grounded him. When it landed, it began to etch the picture of a child's hand-drawn sun, a circle with vibrant beams shooting from it like an early hieroglyph. The circle was empty, but there was nothing grave and impassable about this emptiness, as the fire around it retained the hope that he would one day be filled.

He was open and you could say that whoever is waiting to be filled walks around with a chest that others can swim in and out of quite easily. That's how you attract magic.

To open oneself is to believe. Believe in what? Luck? Miracles? Of course. There are always miracles. Take a breath. See? A miracle. And there's always luck, although we are often unaware of its presence and Ansley was no exception. He was completely naive of the gifts given to him.

He simply walked down the steps of the National Gallery and headed north. He needed trees. He was tired and wanted to be close to something alive. He walked for a long time and when the sun began to peek over the horizon he found a park and an abandoned ice cream van.

It was parked under a large shady yew tree whose boughs extended like arms you'd drag across the ground. He kicked the door in, brushed the mouse droppings away, and curled up under the countertop. He slept through the day and stirred again at sunset with a terrible cramp in his neck. He left the van and sat underneath the large tree. It offered shelter and comfort inside a cloudy dusk. He was still exhausted. He thought he might be tired for the rest of his life and leaned against the tree and shut his eyes.

He didn't realize the significance of the place. How could he? He was emotionally spent. Within minutes he was asleep.

That was luck.

And the beetles crawled out to greet him. They were a miracle.

***

Ansley was the perfect host. He stayed indoors, which was wonderful as the beetles had a tendency to overheat and hated to photosynthesize. He kept a regular diet and was contemplative with the constitution of a marble floor that the beetles loved to roll up and ping against.

***

When he woke up he heard small clicking noises. At first he thought it was an old door gradually popping open like the spine of a book that's been closed for years. Then he heard the earth shuffling and as his eyes adjusted he noticed the beetles. They were all around him, flat as black seeds and reflecting the moon inside them as if they were dropped pupils. Which is to say there was something human about them, yet he didn't feel frightened. He just pushed them away and surveyed his surroundings.

The park seemed empty. There was a stream that fed a lake in the middle with reeds around it and the movement of uneaten ducks. That wasn't surprising as he'd heard that most of London's water fowl had been contaminated. The ducks flapped and quacked reassuringly. He thought of finding a place to live near the ducks so that he might take solace in hearing them.

He walked on and found a graveyard. Most of the graves were incredibly old and damp. The names of their occupants were unintelligible through the moss and when he tried to scrape the moss away, so that he might read them better, bits of stone crumpled under his fingernails, so he stopped.

Brambles covered most of the graves, nettles and woody plants like buddleia. Trees were scattered everywhere. Trees with ivy and fragrant white roses growing up them. It seemed as though the tombstones were misplaced, as if they'd dropped from the sky and landed in woodland. The stone angels, crosses, griffins, and enormous spherical shapes were all adorned with layers of bird droppings thick as candle wax and sat hidden, leaning behind trees. In the center of the graveyard was a huge yew tree with nothing growing beneath it. It was completely untangled, a breathing space, with boughs that dropped like giants arms to the soft needled ground. It seemed to want to offer a lift on its bicep. Birds and butterflies were everywhere. He was amazed at the fortitude of insects, and where there are insects there are birds and where there are birds there are cats.

When he left the graveyard and continued down the pavement to the high street he noticed the cats were everywhere. Shop windows were broken or boarded. A few people looked out and stared at him in amazement. Perhaps they thought he'd come from the crypt. He tended to get that reaction. Eventually he found what he'd been looking for, an empty jar.

He walked back to the park towards the pond. The wind picked up and rustled the leaves of an old willow tree and beneath it he saw that there was a worn boat house. He crossed his fingers that it was empty. He edged his way down the side of the muddy bank and peered around the front.

"Hello?" He called out into the watery darkness. Nothing answered.

It was actually quite a big space. He climbed back up the bank, walked around the other side, and kicked the little door in. A pair of small eyes looked up at him, but it was only a duck on a nest.

"We can share this space," he told her. It still had little steps on either side of the water. Its arches were composed of solid, mossy bricks without a single stream of light filtering through. He'd be safe. He could use the boards from the shop windows to put across the steps, fix the door, and board up the opening from the water as well. Perhaps he might even find a little boat. It would be too cold for the winter but for now it was perfect, plus there were plenty of bugs around.

On his way back to the high street to collect the boards he stopped to pick some caterpillars he'd seen on a patch of nettles earlier. He put them in the jar. Protein. He didn't know when he'd find his next meal. Time to begin his pantry he thought. It was a trick he had learned from his father. The life of an insect is generally too short for BSE to metabolize. If you see bugs on a plant it's a pretty sure bet that the plant is uncontaminated, so gobble up your meal in one, protein and vegetable. He didn't know how long he'd have to observe plants before he knew what he could and couldn't eat. He stuck some beetles in the jar for good measure. He didn't know they were they kind that fed upon the dead.

Days went by and one by one the ducks died. Ansley was afraid to eat anything surrounding the pond. The beetles were still following him everywhere. Sometimes he worried that he might be going mad, that it was too late, that he hadn't been careful enough about what he was eating. The beetles seemed to be listening to him. What was there to hear? He hadn't spoken to anyone in ages. He was hungry and they were multiplying. He picked one up and looked at it.

"If you're a shape-shifter, come out and say it, otherwise I'm going to eat you," he said. The beetle didn't move.

"I'm counting to ten and then popping you in my mouth okay?"

He counted and then nothing happened so he popped it in his mouth. The hard shell before the goo was less than pleasant but it filled the space inside his stomach. Think of it as a treat, a delicacy, he told himself. He was sick of caterpillar. At least beetles were crunchy, besides hunger outweighs disgust. He didn't realize they were carrion beetles until he started hallucinating.

11

She stood up and sat down next to him in the boathouse. Ansley put his hand out and his hand went straight through her figure. He closed and then opened his eyes again. It was still there, or rather, she.

"You're dead," he said, and pointed at her. His finger disappeared into her arm.

"Been longer dead than living sweetheart," she said.

"What are you?"

"I, young man, am an actress!" She spun around, pirouetted, and bowed. "But I'm also a messenger, just until I hit the big time, it's like a day job. My name is Nelly."

Nelly had bobbed blond hair and bright red lipstick. She wore a tasseled purple flapper dress and a peacock feather behind her ear. She looked the image of the roaring twenties.

"Oookaaay but why are you here, bothering me?"

"Oh it's no bother sweetness. You ate my beetle."

"What?"

"My beetle, poor soul, I used to call him Pupil. Do us a favor and open up your mouth," she said, as she stepped closer.

Ansley opened up his mouth and she peered in, shifting her feet to get a better look. Her head disappeared into his as though it were a cloud.

"Pupil honey? You in there? It's all right, Nelly's here now. Don't you worry," she said, and stepped back.

"What the hell is going on?! Who are you speaking to?!"

"Stop shouting at me and listen. I already told you, my beetle, my *carri*on beetle. Pupil ate the whole of my heart, greedy lil' bugger, anyway we can't be separated now. Not for love nor money. And you ate Pupil, so now you're stuck with me. But don't worry, I'm often on tour, so you won't see much of me. Right, speaking of my vocation, I'm off. I've got a gig tonight. Don't look so shocked. Dead people still require entertainment lovey. Don't wait up for me. Get some rest and tomorrow we'll find you a better place to live. There's a container opening up at Big Yellow. A man like you needs to be dry," she said, and nodded towards his notebooks.

He had often worried about the effect of the damp walls on his paper and was grateful for help. "That would be great, thank you."

"Oh, I almost forgot. I have a message for you," she said.

"A message, from who?"

"Whom. I don't know, I'm just the messenger, like I said."

"How can you not know? You saw them didn't you?"

"Her. It's a her, but she's always changing from one thing to the next. She has the light of the angels though."

"So I have a message from an angel?" He was seriously skeptical, but Nelly hardly noticed.

"Yeah, maybe. Hard to say. That's not really my scene," she said.

"So what is it?" He asked, and she cleared her throat ready for the announcement.

"Quote. They are coming for you. Do what they ask and you will be rewarded. Unquote," she saluted and disappeared.

"Wait! Who is coming?!" But she had flown through the wall and was gone.

Ansley stared after her in silence, then he got up and walked along the cemetery. He went through the iron railings and a line of lime trees. He searched through the ferns and sure enough he came across the gravestone of Nelly. It was covered, choked almost in holly and wild heart's tongue.

***

He probably wouldn't have survived the first few months if it weren't for Nelly. She came and went as she pleased and, although it took him a long time to admit it, he missed her when she was gone. She kept her promise and moved him into a Big Yellow storage container. She had her theater troupe scout for paper and soon he had stacks of the stuff and poems tacked all over his walls. And all the while he never forgot the message. Who was coming for him?

12

The lock on Ansley's door was easy enough for Beatrice to pick. Oren, suitably impressed, gave a nod of admiration and cautiously followed her inside. The light from the doorway was the only light in the room and when the door was shut it was completely black.

"Actually Oren, keep it open will you? It's too dark in here otherwise."

The room was windowless and smelled disgustingly sweet like a cave full of bats.

"God this room could use some air. Doesn't he bathe?" Oren pinched his nose with his fingers.

"He's homeless you idiot," snapped Beatrice.

"I thought we just picked the lock to his house?"

"Look around. Does this look like a house to you? It's some kind of storage vault or something," said Beatrice. "Imagine living like this."

"There's the smelly culprit," Oren pointed to a makeshift commode in the corner.

"At least he's not dumping it on the street like everyone else. That's the problem with a water shortage, no flush, no shower."

"Yeah I know. I hate to see people living like animals," he said.

"But he's not. Have you seen the walls? They're alive with words and color."

Beatrice walked up to a poem nailed to the wall and written on the back of a used envelope. She read it out loud:

Foxes
I'd love to follow my nose through the dark,
and zip the night up around me
quick as impulses, fire,
inescapable fear, I live within this frontier.
While beyond, a wilderness sharpens
its blade of evisceration light –
my imagination –
That human splice dividing us from foxes –
But wouldn't it be grand?
Alas, dreams.
Those hidden dens.

"Holy shit, that's absolutely beautiful," she said.

She walked around the room, quietly reading and touching the little fragments of life she came across, ribbons, old ticket stubs, and crumpled pieces of cellophane. The walls were papered with his collection and his words.

"Why does he put all these things on his walls anyway?" said Oren.

"I don't know, maybe it's how he stays sane. You know what it's like when you haven't been outside for ages, how crazy it can make you? Imagine never seeing the sun, never feeling the sun. It's just unthinkable. I mean, look at this, it's some old thank-you card or greeting card or whatever, but he's ripped off the front so that he can hang a bouquet of flowers on his wall." She touched an embossed yellow rose on the card. She realized its hue was tainted brown from his finger rubbings. She turned to Oren.

"Actually, I think we should go. This feels way too private. We shouldn't be here. I don't want him to find us here."

"You were just reading his innermost poetic thoughts a moment ago and now you want to wait outside?"

"Yes and I regret that now. It feels like, I don't know, like we've uncovered an ancient ceremonial ground or something."

"He's not a Neanderthal you know."

"I didn't say that. Now come on."

Out on the street, words, his words, kept repeating in her mind. Zipping up the night. Evisceration light. Those hidden dens. She squinted down the alleyway as if the sight of him might produce a glare. She didn't expect him to be so human, but why? When she was a child his name was synonymous with ghost. She remembered how he was talked about as if he were a curse, of course these ideas are ridiculous but they had obviously left their imprint all the same.

There was something else about the room that had touched her, it was private, it was a home. She'd been running since she was a child. First to Rye and then with her leopard. She had never stayed anywhere long enough to make it personal and now she was remembering so much more about her childhood. She felt longing. A longing for normalcy. She laughed. She was sure he would not describe his existence as normal but what she meant was that his space identified him. His space was like his thumbprint. A creative womb.

She reached her hand inside her knapsack and touched a feather. Her feathers were a form of housekeeping. She'd traveled with her protector like birds following the magnetic forces of the earth. Around and around they went never leaving a trace. The feathers were light. What else could she take? She'd been collecting them for as long as she could remember. It was her way of harvesting freedom. Often she would take a single bird's quill and stroke its spine until each individual feather was pointing in the same direction like an arrow. It calmed her. It kept her from pulling her hair out. Most of the feathers she found were mangy and blood stained. Only the seabirds' feathers were untouched and in beautiful condition. Though they were not in abundance. She kept them in her knapsack, rolled in a towel, which she also used as a pillow. Before she went to sleep she asked her birds to look after her. She often dreamt that she could fly. Which was why it was surprising that her protector was a leopard, surprising in a lovely way that meant the birds were her insight alone, her guardians of choice, not just another duty.

Soon they would offer Ansley the choice to join their mission. He could say no. This fact enthralled her. All her life she'd been bound by a single great obligation, whereas Ansley was free, wasn't he? She wondered as she peered down the alleyway, waiting, and straining to see him.

13

When the Growers found him he'd been living in an abandoned storage warehouse in London near the river. He had subsisted on rats, not the white ones of course, the white ones reminded him too much of himself.

The night they came, he'd been walking the fires, as was his custom, looking for something. What exactly? It's hard to explain, a representation, a symbol. Once he found a picture of a family smiling like a rainbow against the gray pavement. He took it home and tacked it on his damp wall. That started his searching for color. He spent his days inside avoiding the sun until night, like a cool sheet, fell as a relief. He left his house with the bats, the fox, the mad and dark shufflers all swirling out like smoke onto the streets. His pallor skin was almost beautiful in the moonlight, tragically beautiful and luminous as a ghost. When he walked he made no noise. Color wasn't his only hunger. He also craved paper, words.

Sometimes he just wanted to see a single word written on a white slice of page. Silver. Silver was such a word. He loved the way it slipped in and out of sliver, which gave way to shiver, so that somehow it managed to be both hot and cold. Words in front or behind it would only muddy its radiance. Some words, like people, are better off alone. Silver Ansley, he thought to himself, a slice of moonlight in a dark alleyway, alone. It rolled across the tongue like a petal blade.

He turned the corner and saw Beatrice before she saw him. He didn't realize who she was as they hadn't actually met when they lived in Rye. It was past midnight and her face was pinched as she stared down the dark street. She had waist-length black hair. She seemed strong and quick and reminded him of a lovely crow. Oren walked around the corner and spoke to her.

Ansley instinctively knew they were looking for him. He placed the tiny red hair clip, that night's found object of color, into his pocket and walked forward. When Beatrice saw him she lifted her arms, almost as if she were going to run and hug him, then stopped herself.

"Can I help you?" Ansley said.

"Ansley right?" she said, and he nodded yes.

She gave a little chuckle and reached out to touch his empty hands. She was bubbling over with exuberance. He couldn't understand why he didn't repel her. Instead they stared at him as if he were something miraculous. There was no malice in their stare.

She had on an army green coat with deep pockets and from one of these pockets she produced a peach, which she held in front of her face and called "a ball of sunrise" before handing it to him. It had been years since he'd held a piece of fruit in his hand. It was incredibly soft, baby soft.

"Breathe it in before you eat it," she said.

He did as he was told and brought it to his nose like a rare flower and breathed. It was exhilarating. He had forgotten how restoring the earth could smell.

"Thank you," he said, and took a bite. It was like tasting a phenomenon.

"You're welcome," Beatrice replied, and touched his arm. Her touch made him flinch as violently as if he'd been slapped.

"I'm sorry, I didn't mean anything," she said, alarmed, and pulled her hand away.

"No. No, it's me, I'm the one who's sorry. That's the sum of my human experience lately I'm afraid," he laughed at his reaction and she nodded solemnly.

"You don't know who I am do you?" Beatrice asked.

"No. I'm sorry I don't," he answered.

"I'm Beatrice. Beatrice Falconer from Rye," she said.

Ansley stepped back and eyed her suspiciously. He had tried to forget his life in Rye.

"Marianne sent me," said Beatrice.

"Marianne?" He was shocked. "But I thought she was, I guess I just assumed she was dead."

"She escaped Ansley," said Beatrice.

"So did Dex," said Oren and Ansley, visibly bristled.

"I see. I can't imagine they'd want me then."

"What? You don't know what you're talking about! They thought that you had died in a fire. They were devastated. I was there when they found out you were alive and they were thrilled, absolutely thrilled, jumping up and down and everything," said Oren.

"I bet," said Ansley sarcastically.

"I'm serious. They sent us to collect you," said Oren.

"Collect me? I'm not a seed you know. Look, I'm sorry, but you've wasted your time. I think you should leave now," he said.

"Why Ansley? What is there here for you?" Beatrice asked.

"Nothing. Which is exactly what I want. Peace and nothing. Besides what do they have for me?"

"A chance actually," she said.

"Chance?! Ha. That's funny. A chance at what exactly?"

"Jude has the pearl," Beatrice said.

"What do you mean? The prophet?"

"Yes, the prophet, who has returned to his snake form, has stolen the pearl, which you know is a seed. And we want to get it back, but we need your help."

"I don't know how I could be of any help," he said.

"Just say you'll help us Ansley. We are running out of time. It will be daylight soon. Please?"

"No."

"Marianne asked me to give this to you," Oren said, and flung the ring towards him. It was his mother's wedding ring. He rolled it around in his hand.

"They went to the fire and found it. She said it's why they thought you were dead. She said they would never have left if they had known you were alive."

"How did they find out I was here?" Ansley asked, without taking his eyes off the ring. It had been so long since he'd touched it, or anyone, or anything meaningful.

"You are never going to believe this but a beetle told them," said Oren.

Ansley looked up at Oren and laughed out loud. Oren and Beatrice looked at one another.

"It's a strange world," Ansley said, still laughing.

"So you'll come?" Beatrice asked.

"It doesn't look like I have much choice," he said.

Which was true. The alternative was to spend his life governed by darkness.

"I just need to get a few things," he said, and went to open the door of the boathouse. He noticed the lock was undone. He turned around and glared at them.

"Have you been in here?" He started walking back towards them.

"Yes and I have to say your poetry is beautiful," Beatrice said impetuously.

Ansley stopped dead in his tracks. She wanted to suck the words back in as soon as she'd said them. She put her foot in her mouth. Aargh!

"Good one," whispered Oren.

Ansley turned to face her. "What did you say?"

"Ansley, I'm so sorry. You see, we, I mean, I picked the lock when you were out. I didn't mean to, to snoop exactly. I just wanted to see if you were in."

"You could have knocked."

"I did! I did knock."

"So you knew I wasn't there and went in anyway?"

"Oh. Well, yes. But if I'd known how, how personal it was, I swear I never would have dreamed of breaking in. Really I am quite a considerate person."

"Obviously."

"No really I made us leave as soon as I read one of your poems. Didn't I Oren?"

"She did. She said it felt too private," said Oren.

"What? You read them?" said Ansley.

"Don't hate me but, yes, I did and they were so moving. I've never read anything so beautiful in my life."

He looked at her and slowly turned and walked towards the door. In a moment he was gone.

"I can't believe I said that. I'm such a jerk," Beatrice whispered to Oren.

"I know."

"We should never have broken into his place. What was I thinking?"

"You weren't."

"What?! You could have stayed behind you know. You're my accomplice so don't act so high and mighty."

"Whatever. Do you think he'll come back out?"

"I'm not sure. Do you think he'll hate me now?"

"Absolutely. In fact, he's probably composing a poem about how much he hates you this instant."

"Oh shut up."

"Anything you say."

14

Ansley entered his room and took a deep breath. She had been in here. It was humiliating. She had touched his things. The lovely little crow had touched his things. Nobody had ever been inside his room before, apart from Nelly. Nobody had ever read his words, since Marianne. She called them moving and beautiful. Maybe she was just being nice. His appearance had probably frightened her into lying. Maybe they won't be there when he returns. Although she did look him right in the eye. The man too, he didn't seem like most men, rather, well, honest. The lovely crow had said his poems were beautiful. He grabbed his poems from the walls, rolled them and secured them with a rubber band. He left without even thinking about his rainbow family. He left them behind. They were never his anyway. When he opened the door to the street the lovely crow turned, her face awash with relief.

"Ansley I'm so glad you decided to come back. We were worried. I can't apologize enough. I promise I'll never invade your privacy again."

"It's okay, honestly, it's fine. I understand. Humans are naturally curious."

"Curiosity killed the cat. Or leopard in Beatrice's case," said Oren, smirking.

"What does he mean?" said Ansley.

"Just don't listen to him. I have a leopard protector is all. But we'll explain that later. Right now we need to walk. I don't want the sun to rise on you Ansley and we need to meet our ride. Here, eat this, it'll keep you going," she said, handing him a banana.

"Are you some sort of fruit hamper?" Ansley said.

Beatrice and Oren looked at one another.

"Yeah, something like that," Oren said, and winked.

"Let's go," Beatrice shouted over her shoulder. She was already halfway down the street.

***

They walked through the night and the fires jumped on the inky streets like mad devils. The bright flowers of graffiti shot against each wall and above them, bullet holes, displayed in patterns like flights of geese. Ansley had survived in the world by kaleidoscoping images until they felt decent. The black sky seemed to fold them inside her wings like a huge oily bird that helped them weave through the city. The moon was too big and clear, so clear the edges appeared hazed and watery as if it were a stone shining up from a colorless pool. As if everything were upside down. He closed his eyes and made a wish and when he opened them, Beatrice was looking up at him, her eyes were full of tenderness. They had reached the edge of the city.

"Have you been out this far?" she said.

"Not in a long time," he said.

Oren nodded towards a large hill and they climbed it. From the top Ansley could see where rabbits had skated across a stretch of endless sand. Beatrice pointed to some scraggly bushes alongside the road and told him they were once hedgerows, before the heat, before the drought it had all been green and yellow fields. Trees grew sideways in the wind, of course that was always the case she explained, first the sea wind, now the sand wind. Eroding and leafless trees rose out of the swirling sand like bony fingers, buffeted and polished. Farmhouses crouched in hills, their windows bricked up like red eyes. Every so often you'd see a lonely pair of rusty gates leading nowhere, as if the house had been swallowed, leaving behind a large bowl shape in the ground. Tree roots, still visible and silver as skinless knuckles banked either side of twisting roads. Ansley couldn't hear a single animal. No machines, no animals, just silence broken only by wind. Yes, he knew the landscape that she was explaining but he wanted to hear her speak, he wanted to hear her shape that world.

"We'll wait here for our ride," she said, and the three of them stared across the scenery. Then Beatrice did something unexpected. She did a little dance. Just like that. A little dance for no recognizable reason. She might be mad and dangerous, he thought, delighted. He looked at her dancing and clapping her hands, definitely mad, but probably not dangerous. He had to smile, though not with his teeth. She caught him smiling and pointed at him, I saw you, I saw you, I saw you shaking her hips with each syllable. She stopped and looked him square in the eye. Hers were a golden green.

"You think I'm crazy. That's okay. I've always wanted to dance on a hilltop under the moonlight. Maybe I was a witch in a past life huh? Besides, if I didn't act a little crazy I'd certainly go crazy. You know what I mean? I'd absolutely tear my hair out," she instantly blushed, realizing he had about five hairs on his head in total.

"Yeah, that's not a problem I have to worry about," he said. He was joking and she laughed but there was sadness in it.

"Can I ask you something? Something personal?" she said.

"Sure," he said.

"Like you could stop her," said Oren, and Beatrice ignored him.

"Did you ever have hair?" she said.

"Never like yours. I used to dream that my hair wouldn't stop growing, that it'd fill the room and I'd have to walk and walk through it to find the door. It was silky as I parted it with my fingers. It wasn't a nightmare or anything. I always woke up soothed and comforted."

She ran her fingers through her hair and looked at it thoughtfully.

"I used to dream that I was a moth that drank from the open mouths of sleeping animals. Every night, escaping jaws. When I woke up I felt powerful," she said, as she fluttered her hands like a moth against the amethyst sky. Dawn was on its way. "Now I understand perfectly."

15

Their arrival was soundless. The moths slowed and formed a large net that gently dropped them to the ground. At once, Ansley recognized the field and the castle that had been bombed to a pile of rubble crumpling in the distance. But there was no sign of the woodland as the South Downs spread uninterrupted before them. It was the quietest time of night, after the nocturnal creatures had retired and before the morning's activity. The three of them stood for a moment inside this stillness.

"Must be strange to be back here huh?" Oren said.

"Yes, but it looks so different now it's hardly recognizable," said Ansley. "It's nothing but field and sky." It struck him that Marianne might be unrecognizable as well and he felt afraid. "So much has vanished," he said, his voice full of meaning.

"Not everything. Just wait. These moths are brilliant at camouflage. They can completely cloak a thing," Oren whispered, and pointed to the middle of the field.

The horizon started to bubble moth wings. Each one a pixel that tore away and en mass ripped a strip down the center of the sky to reveal the beech tree.

Beatrice gasped. "There it is," she said, awestruck.

It was magnificent, huge, and levitating. Its roots spread as wide as its branches, where the leaves were green and fuming with smoke like the Growers' seeds.

"It's in the same place," said Ansley. "It looks as though its sucked up all the silver water and grown," he wondered if he were the only one that had been living a stagnant life.

"It's the color of you," said Beatrice.

Which was true. Its bark was smooth moonlit silver that looked like a marble tower to the clouds. Their eyes followed it up.

"Where does it end?" said Beatrice

"Maybe it doesn't," said Oren, as he approached the tree, stuck his finger under one of its many grooves of bark, and lifted.

The bark broke away and exposed a doorknob. Oren turned it and the tree opened. Inside was a small dark vault.

Ansley and Beatrice looked at one another in surprise.

"You just put your hand anywhere inside the bark and if it recognizes you as a friend, a doorknob will appear," said Oren, stepping inside the vault as though it were an elevator shaft. "Come on."

"Recognizes you as a friend," Ansley repeated what Oren had said, "you mean, like intuition? Are you telling me this tree has a conscience?"

"Of course it has a conscience, it's alive," said Oren, moving to the side so that Ansley could enter the vault.

Beatrice joined them. "It's probably more alive than we are," she said.

"You mean aware," said Ansley.

"What's the difference?"

Ansley shrugged. Perhaps awareness was the only true marker for life, certainly conscious life, and this tree seemed as alert as anything he had ever known. The air was moist and spongy fresh inside the bark vault. There was just enough room for the three of them to stand. One by one the pixel moths hid the tree and rebuilt the picture of undulating metallic sky. They were trapped inside the tree and it was completely dark. It felt as though the tree was smelling them, listening, when something rough scraped down Ansley's arm.

"Hey!" he shouted.

"Shh," said Oren. "It's okay, it's just judging us."

Thin layers of bark frisked over their bodies, it was scratchy and uncomfortable, but painless. When the tree was satisfied, it drew the bark back into its cavity and a single moth lit its abdomen, like a tiny ceiling lantern.

Their figures were barely visible and their combined breath made a tangy smell. It was getting awkward, for to move was to touch one another.

"Now what?" Ansley asked, his mouth watering with panic.

"Now it gets interesting," said Oren. "This is how it works. The entry is open for interpretation, which means in order to see an opening, you have to close your eyes and visualize one," Oren said.

"Can we visualize anything?" Beatrice said.

"Anything. I promise it works. Ready?"

"Ready," said Beatrice, and Ansley nodded, he felt like he was dreaming.

Beatrice closed her eyes and saw a dimly lit glass tube. On the other side of the glass were ants, beetles, ladybugs, wood lice, and mice curled up in the bark. She saw sleeping owlets and birds of every size and color. She grabbed Ansley's hand and together they ran through the tube. Their feet made small thuds against the glass. Behind them the doorway shifted into another place and melted into the bark.

Ansley's visualization came from a dark corner, it came easily. He saw a doorway. It was the threshold to the poet's house. In his mind he ran, as he had done a million times before, through the slant of sunlight on the stone floor. He ran out into the open day, bright as a peeled orange, he ran to Marianne. Her hair in the sunlight was a curtain of iridescent feathers. Her smile. Only this time, his chest pounded, this time she'll be waiting. She'll be real, he thought. The words:

A growling hurt
Makes the heart grow rabid
Like entering a room
You know you'll never
Leave.

16

Time and retrospection had reduced his loss to accountable digits. He died, she died, everything fell on these dates, etc. But the unaccountable things, like chances, were odds that still stilted him. What if she hadn't? What if he hadn't? How would he have kept life afloat? So that his history was boxed into categories of "what was" and "what might have been" and the loss of a different outcome, a different pathway eventually became the loss of all possibility, all hope for a future. The expectation of loss had become his truth. It ached in him immeasurably like a dream that could not be caught or stopped; it bedded down and planted its deadening relic.

And yet. Now. The chance to reshape what he assumed had been forged, the chance to live a different path, again.

The stakes of this pierced his chest and he could barely breathe, as if breath were secondary to pain.

They came to a pale lilac curtain of moths, wing touching wing and completely still, a warm light diffused through their tissue-paper wings. Oren moved the curtain aside and the moths tinkled as if they were frozen. A circular wooden room was unveiled. The bark walls were a coppery red and springy to touch, yet as smooth as cloth, upon which vines and flowers were carved so delicately they appeared to be stitched. Inside the center of the larger flowers were brightly lit opals that made the room glow. On the floor was a crucifix composed of four golden leaves and Marianne stood in the middle, where everything joined, Ansley thought and felt himself slipping. Her eyes were closed as though she were meditating.

There she was, like a dream, like a ghost, and he thought for a moment that maybe he swallowed her beetle. He watched her for a few milliseconds and tried to stop his eyes from shining into her, to stop his brute presence from being felt so that he could just observe her, privately, as one observes art. But the pause was terrible for its intensity, like knowing you have to do something makes it more difficult to begin and he felt relieved with she opened her eyes and beheld him.

She looked dusted in silver, her hair, her skin, her eyes and their lashes as if she'd been powdered with moonlight. Moths spun in slow circles around her head. She lifted her hand and moths dropped down from the ceiling and haloed the heads of Ansley and the Growers. Above them, thousands of moths coated the ceiling with their slightly fanning wings as though they were awaiting instruction.

A small cry escaped her mouth and she ran towards him.

To suddenly be awash with her body, crushed by her hair, her scent was more than he could handle and his knees began to give way. The air was water he was falling through.

"You're alive!" she pressed her hands against his cheeks and rubbed his bald head, hugging him over and over again. And he thought:

The time before
And the time after
Seems at once both
Meaningless and prophetic
Now that you're here
Touching me
And I, you.

"So it's true," she finally let him go. "You're alive. I refused to believe it until I saw you, I didn't want to allow false hope."

Her fingers had left a trail of moth dust on his balaclava. "But here you are," she murmured, drew him near, and held him tight once more.

She was different now, a woman, not the girl he'd remembered and hologrammed in his mind as perfect. Who was this? Even her eyes were star studded and trickling with life. He felt dead by comparison.

"I've missed you," she said, nuzzling into his chest.

The powder of her filled his nostrils, he breathed her in, she smelt of the night and he recognized himself in her scent. He couldn't think.

"I can't believe you're alive," she said, as she let go of him and placed her hands on Oren's shoulders. "Welcome back. Thank you for showing them the way," she said, squeezed him, and kissed his cheeks. "And Beatrice," she turned and cupped the girl's chin in her soft hand. "If I would have known that you were alive I would have searched everywhere for you. We thought Jude had taken you, I'm so sorry," she said.

"It's okay. It was planned this way," said Beatrice.

"I know. But all the same, I would have found you," she said, and turned to Ansley. "And you. If we had believed even for a second that you were alive," her voice snagged on emotion.

"We," thought Ansley, she said "we" and that meant Dex. Her eyes were watery and held his gaze until he looked away.

Throughout the years his mind had become a deserted mine. It was too dangerous for his whole person to traverse, but he let his poems enter. They flitted down each shaft like a single white snowflake, illuminating chamber by chamber, until they melted into blackness. Sometimes what he wrote was unrecognizable, yet his words could fill him and he knew, instinctively, that he was living close to his true self, from which everything else grew. He knew he was living his soil. The part of himself that he'd buried her inside.

What else could he have done? But kill her in his mind?

He laid her gently inside one of his chambers, let the snow of himself fall and melt poems into parts of her. Her black hair, her thighs, the dip of her collarbone, her lips. In that way, she'd remained his. But it was all past tense, how they'd felt, what they'd shared was history, yet all the while she'd been creating something new. With Dex.

The betrayal choked him. She touched him again and he shoved her hand away.

"I thought you were dead," he managed to say, a film of vomit on his tongue.

Why aren't you dead? He thought. It would be easier somehow, as though he'd won, instead he'd lost her to Dex. There was love between them and things he'd never understand or know because she'd become a woman in Dex's presence. And quite possibly, in his embrace.

"We thought you were dead too mate," said Dex, stepping into the room.

He looked the same only older, thinner. His blond curls still dangled aloof and unkempt. His skin was even darker in mothlight. Ansley hated how casual he could be, hated the admiration he felt steaming off Beatrice and Oren, hated that Dex could walk up behind Marianne and rest his hand on her shoulder like a claim that fit.

But it was the word "mate" that unhinged Ansley.

He sprang towards Dex with the bellow of an animal. Marianne screamed and fell to the ground and within seconds Ansley had his hands around Dex's neck.

"Don't you ever call me mate!" Ansley spat, and tightened his hands around Dex's throat.

Dex gagged as Ansley shoved him to the ground by punching a knee into his stomach. Dex was no match for the survival skills Ansley had learned while living on the London streets. Dex's face was turning purple. Ansley's teeth were yellow and sharp as broken glass. He wanted to bite into Dex. He wanted to bite his perfect face, chew it, and spit it out. His pink eyes were red and vivid with anger.

"Stop it!" Marianne shouted, and flung herself on top of them. "You'll kill him! Shift!"

Dex listened, shifted into a blackbird and flew to a perch on the ceiling.

"You stole her!" Ansley screamed, while Marianne held onto his shoulders. "You stole her from me!" He broke into a sob and pushed Marianne away.

"I loved you," he cried, and collapsed on the ground like a broken machine. "You knew I loved you and still ..." he couldn't continue.

There was only his sobbing and the calm beating of wings inside silence. Eventually Marianne knelt beside him, whispered in his ear, and raised her hand. A net of glowing moths dropped from the ceiling, cocooned around Ansley and carried him up a spiral staircase built along the curvature of the tree trunk. Marianne slowly followed them up the stairs under a moth halo. She didn't even glance at Dex. When she was out of view, Beatrice looked at Oren with stunned disbelief.

"Damn," Oren made a low whistling sound. "I certainly didn't see that coming."

"I know," said Beatrice. "Poor Ansley." She looked in the direction of the stairs.

"You hungry?" Oren asked.

"Come to think of it I am," she said.

"Well let's take our hamper selves into the kitchen and see what we can doctor up," he said.

Dex watched from the shadowed rafters like an afterthought, then descended, flew through the moth curtain and out into the night.

17

He shifted into a fox and ran for miles. His feet pounded against the heather and the dry soil. Above the moon was glaring, laughing at him. He saw the blue fires in the distance and ran towards them. The stone pub was nestled into the side of the Downs like a wart under a cheekbone. A man was in the window watching and when he saw him approach, the man went to the door and called out to Dex.

"You, fox, come here!" He shouted.

Dex went closer. Close enough to feel the heat rolling out of the doorway. Close enough to see the man. He was gray as though he'd been drained. Only the cracks in his lips were red. He had a patch across one eye and the other was huge and lashless. Dex expected him to shift into an owl. He bared his teeth at the man and growled.

"Stop that foolishness and come out of yourself boy," the man said.

Dex just stared at him. How did he know?

"Yes, yes. I know you're in there," he said, and opened the door wide so that Dex could come inside.

Dex followed him but he did not shift. The room was full of empty old tables and chairs. The fire was roaring, suffocating the room. The man walked behind the counter and pulled himself a pint of lager. He drank it down noisily in a few gulps. His chin glistened with spit.

"Ahhh that's better," he said, and ran his hand over his mouth, then through his greasy hair.

Dex looked for an open window or a place to escape. How could he have been so foolish? He thought to himself.

"Don't you worry lad. I'm not here for the likes of you. I'm repaying a debt see. I'll tell you about it, sure I will, but are you going to, what do you call it, change?"

Dex shook his pointy-eared head. No. He could go for the throat as a fox, but not as a human.

"Very well then. That must be your true nature. I know all about nature, isn't it wonderful? Especially snakes. I loved them until I spent time in one," he leaned forward and looked at Dex hard. "In *him*. I was in*side him*," he paused as though the memory were painful.

"I was a naturalist. Hard to believe right? Hard to believe when you see me now. I look dead because I am. I got mean and that's a form of death. And then he swallowed me. Whole. Living inside that, that 'thing' almost killed all the good in me. Almost. I got something for you," he said, and lifted the patch over his eye.

Under it was a gold coin. He winked and the coin popped out and landed on his palm.

"Take it. It got me out of him alive. You're going to see him soon and there will be a battle. Give it back to him," he said, threw the coin up into the air and Dex caught it in his mouth.

"Tell him I don't want it anymore. That there are worse things than dying. There's death on the inside. There's living without love. But you know all about that now don't you? Don't look so surprised. I know things. I create things. You think this pub exists?" He snapped his fingers and the two of them were standing alone on a windblown hill.

"See my power? Watch this," he snapped his fingers and they were back inside the pub.

"I can get rid of him, the one they call Dark Ansley. Whenever you want, lickety-split, you just return that coin for me and say the word. I'll be here pouring pints," he said, and smiled.

Suddenly there were people everywhere, laughing and pointing at him. He could see the fire flickering through their bodies. They were transparent, ghosts, and Nelly was one of them. She had heard everything.

"Go on! Get!" The man shouted and clapped his hands.

Dex ran towards the door. The man followed.

"Remember," he whispered, as he pushed open the door. "I'm always around."

Dex took one last look at him and ran out into the night. Nelly finished her drink and flew through the wall after Dex.

The coin was clenched in his sharp teeth.

It was an obol. A coin to pay Charon.

18

Simorg had been just a boy the first time he met Jude. A boy who had been dared to enter a water pipe and hadn't seen the man crawling about twenty feet ahead of him. Simorg's eyes were still blinded from the sunlight and his chest was still engorged from the dare. This would be a dare to beat all others. It would be legendry, he thought, and to be legendry you have to be brave. He only had to crawl through the pipe for two minutes. History is often made in a matter of minutes, he reminded himself, and he could hear his friends counting.

There had always been something evil about the pipe, strange, unaccountable noises and meaty, metallic smells. But more than that. Something spectral, that they couldn't name, a terror that they couldn't hear, a silent scream. It was said that sometimes the water dripped red. The grownups said it was simply rust, but the children believed it was blood and the pipe was a passageway to hell.

Simorg's brain mimicked the buzz of the water-treatment plant. His jeans were soaked to his knees but he kept crawling. The light from the entrance began to fade along with the voices of his friends. Small stones embedded into his water-soft palms and he kept stopping to pick them out like picking pebbles out of play dough.

It was then that he heard the man's rhythmical splashing. Simorg stopped moving but his heart began to race. Someone else was in the pipe. He looked down, the water was still clear and foamy. Maybe it was just an animal? Oh my God what if it was a rat? Didn't rats corner people and maul them? He thought of the honey sandwich he'd eaten earlier, sitting at his lovely wooden kitchen table and off a plate with his name on it. His mother had ruffled his hair. He licked his lips and could actually taste the remnants of honey. The rat would start with his lips.

There was a loud bang followed by cursing. That's no rat, thought Jude, but it might be a murderer. What would a murderer be doing in a water pipe? Hiding a body of course. And then to prove his point a pair of shoes came tumbling towards him and he gasped. The man heard his gasp and immediately stopped.

"Who's there?" he shouted.

Simorg could just make out his profile in the dark. He seemed to be without a nose. Their shadows made the water black water and it rocked between them.

"I, I'm sorry?"

"Sorry? That's your name?" He spoke as though he were shouting a song.

"No, but, but O God don't kill me!" Simorg began to softly whimper.

"Silence!"

Simorg suppressed his crying by biting his tongue. His mouth filled with blood. The walls of the pipe were dripping against his hair. A dollop of water slid down his forehead, past his nose, off the slope of his top lip, and into his mouth. It tasted of metal. Water had completely saturated his trouser legs and his jeans were wet and heavy. In the distance, as far away as a dream, he could hear his friends still counting.

"That's better. Now. I'm not going to kill you," Jude said.

"Thank you," Simorg could breathe again.

"But!"

"But?"

"You are a plump little billy goat aren't you?"

Simorg was too scared to answer.

"I said, aren't you!"

"Yes! Yes I am, I, I, I like to eat."

"Hmmmm. So do I. So do I."

Simorg noticed for the first time a thin film around the pipe between himself and the man. It had a dull shimmer almost as if a broken spider's web was hanging from the metal. A piece detached and slowly fell against Simorg's cheek like a wet leaf. It was thicker than a web. He peeled it off with his thumb and forefinger. A residue remained on his cheek and when he tried to rub it off it balled up as if he'd been rubbing glue off his fingers. He could feel the man watching him.

"Not fond of me, eh?"

"I don't know you Sir."

"Yes you do," he laughed, and his laugh vibrated like an ear-splitting bell. "Cool it with the Sir," he said. "Why are you here? Did they send you?"

"No. Nobody sent me. I'm here on a bet. It was just a dare."

"A bet! Ha Ha Ha!" He rang out, when he laughed he threw his bald head back and his black coat fell from his shoulders. He had no arms. Simorg tried not to stare. His shoulders were rounded off as smooth as billiard balls.

"A bet, O Jesus, I've made a few of those!" He carried on laughing. "That's perfect, just perfect. So why don't you run?"

"I have to stay for two minutes. It's a dare."

"You're proud. I like that. I'm proud too, see? I knew you knew me."

He turned and faced Simorg and Simorg could see his eyes reflecting like two golden coins at the bottom of a dark well. Suddenly Simorg was overcome with the desire to touch him and, like a child, wanted to collect the coins from the bottom of the well. He was that shiny, that forbidden and tempting.

"Whatever you wish," Jude said slowly, knowingly. "I can give you whatever you wish. Take the coins."

"What? How did you know?"

"I know everything. Here they come."

He heard splashing and banging. The metal pipe vibrated.

"Si?! You can come out now! Come on this isn't funny! You win, okay? You are the bravest of the brave! You're the master! Come on!" It was his friends.

"The master, hmmm, nice isn't it? To be master," Jude said, as he slid forward. He was not a man at all. Simorg backed up against the cool and gritty pipe. "But you're a, a, what are you?!"

"I am everything," His eyes were watery pools and his pupils were golden coins. "Go on, take one," he said.

Without thinking Simorg reached into his eye and took a coin. The water was like normal water, but freezing cold. The coin was heavy.

"Good boy," he laughed. "Good boy. Now go! Go!" He screamed and opened his mouth as wide and round as the tunnel.

Simorg saw two fangs as large as elephant tusks. He couldn't move. He seemed paralyzed. Inside the snake's red mouth, taunt as a muscle, laid a white arm, dead and grotesque as a fingernail on a tongue. The snake had been swallowing a body.

"Dead," breathed Simorg. "He's dead."

But then the fingers flicked open and the hand reached up and grabbed one of the fangs, pulling its crushed body behind it.

"The coin," the bartender had whispered. White pus sputtered from his mouth. "Give me the coin."

Simorg tossed him the coin and he caught it with the hand that gripped the fang. He slowly folded back into the red muscle.

"I'll find you. Thank you." Simorg heard him whisper.

The snake snapped his mouth shut and became man sized again. He didn't realize the man he'd been swallowing was alive.

"What's this? You want to stay with me? I don't often give chances, but I see power in you, control." Jude whipped his tail forward like a lasso and snared Simorg's wrist. He stuck one of his scales, black and shiny, into his fat palm and it immediately disappeared. "A present," he hissed. "I might need you later."

"No, no," Simorg stumbled backwards and tried to turn around but was stuck against the bartender's shoes. They were black and looked expensive. He could hear his friends coming closer.

"Turn back!" He shouted at them. "Run away!"

"Si is that you? Come out!"

"Run away!" He shouted, and thought he could hear them leaving the pipe.

Simorg finally dislodged the shoes from under his bottom and, scraping his shoulder against the pipe, turned his body and scurried away. He could hear the snake's tail whipping against the pipe as it chased him. He could see the entrance of the pipe, a lit circle, round as the sun with the black silhouettes of his friends bobbing inside it. Faster and faster he crawled while the tail smacked behind him. His palms and knees were bleeding. His shoulder hurt like something fierce. Finally he was within flinging distance of the entrance, so thrust his body forwards, shoving his arms through the light.

"Help me!"

His friends immediately grabbed his hands, and just as he felt a cold current coil around his legs, they pulled him through the tunnel like a wet lamb.

"What the hell?" They said, staring at him in disbelief.

"What the hell is all over you? Is it, like, glue?"

Simorg pulled himself up. He looked at his arms. They were covered in a white sap with bits of rock and grit rolled inside it like fossils. He turned and looked at the water pipe. A stream of water trickled out of its mouth, but other than that it was completely silent.

"You scared us," his friends said, and he just nodded.

He had scared himself, he thought, and there was a part of him that had liked it.

19

The moths gently dropped Ansley on the bed and Marianne sat beside him. The room was empty, but for a dresser with a clay pitcher of water on top of it and a bar of soap. There were no windows. The walls were made of smooth wood with a patterned grain swept up in a curve like a giant bent bough.

Ansley crawled between the white bed linen and closed his eyes. He was tired, but far from sleep. He just wanted to remain completely still. He wasn't ready to speak to Marianne and turned away from her. He could feel the tree's life throbbing as though he were inside a large artery. He let the throbbing overtake him and he breathed. He tucked his legs up under his chin. If he thought it would help, he'd cry again.

Seeing Marianne had been blissful agony. He hadn't realized how much he'd missed her until she was right in front of him and the anger he'd thought had dissipated, felt renewed. But did he still care for her or was he just angry about the life he'd lost? She was beautiful, yes, but she had changed, quite literally. He didn't know this version of Marianne, she was no longer recognizable, nor was Dex. The fact that they had moved forward and grown together without him was the most painful thing of all. He had been too busy surviving to even consider metamorphosing. He was still the same. Nothing. Remarkable in all the wrong ways and hidden.

"Ansley," she put her hand on his back, her deliberation filled the room. "Ansley, I'm so sorry," she said. "You have no idea how difficult it's been."

"No," he said, turning to face her. "*You* have no idea how difficult it's been."

"But I want to. I want to know everything that's happened to you over the last few years. I want our friendship back. I meant it when I said that I've missed you."

"You're with Dex now Marianne. How can you say this? What do you want me to do? Ignore my feelings and watch you two together?"

"No, no, of course not," she put her head in her hands.

"I'm exhausted," he said. "I just want to be left alone."

"I understand," she said, and rose to leave. "We can talk in the morning. I know you might not believe this, but it is wonderful to have you here, it really is."

She stood looking at him before she closed the door. Her cheeks were hollow in the mothlight, her face was drawn, and Ansley thought he could see the woman she would age into. It occurred to him that he wanted to be there to witness this transformation. He loved her still.

"Goodnight," she said, as she closed the door. The hope and tenderness in her voice made Ansley cringe.

"So that's her is it?" Nelly came out of the corner and Ansley groaned. "That's the woman you're risking my Pupil for? She seems a bit powdery and flimsy to me," she hovered next to Ansley.

"Coming from one who is completely see-through," Ansley said.

"Don't be mean. You know that's just circumstantial. There'll never be a more solid woman than yours truly," she air punched him on the chin. "Open up."

"No," he said.

"Go on, open," she said.

"I assume that you eavesdropped during our conversation, so you must have heard me say that I want to be left alone," he said.

"Not until you open," she said.

"Fine," he said, and opened his mouth wide.

Nelly peered down and waved at Pupil and Ansley chomped his jaws shut.

"Boy you are grumpy," she said. "I half thought you'd be happy to see me since you think of me as your mother and all," she said as she lay down beside him and air stroked his hair.

He snorted at her comment. "More like dysfunctional aunt," he said.

"Now that's nice," she said, without a hint of sarcasm in her voice, and Ansley rolled his eyes.

"How did you find me anyway? I thought you were on tour?"

"Well. There's a story. I was minding my own business, having a little gin break, when this fox strolled in."

"You mean Dex?"

"I don't know who it was, but your name was mentioned, or rather, your head."

"My head?"

"The bartender is a bit of a dark agent. He gave the fox a coin and told him he would get rid of you if the fox delivered the coin to its owner."

Ansley thought of the coin Jude had given him. He had sewn it into the hem of his jacket. What were these coins?

"Why would Dex need to get rid of me?"

"Don't be daft. Because of the girl, obviously, Little Miss Fairy Wings."

"She doesn't want me."

"She doesn't know what she wants, believe me."

"What do I do?"

"The first thing you do is stop worrying and moaning about all and sundry. I can't stand to think of Pupil suffering your indigestion. As for foxy, leave it with me and I'll keep an eye on him," she said, blew him a kiss, and melted into the wall.

20

Beatrice was in the bedroom beside Ansley's. It was square with smooth bark walls and a wooden floor. A thick branch protruded from the floor and split like a Y before it ascended out of the wooden shingled roof. From it hung a small lantern. The moths from her halo filled the lantern with light. They had unpacked her things. There was a bookcase full of her books and a wardrobe with her two shirts and jeans hanging inside.

In the corner of the closet she noticed a few pots of paint and a paintbrush. She hung up her jacket and sat down on the bed. It was luxuriously large with feather down pillows and duvet. She sunk into it with her clothes on and pulled the covers up to her chin.

She thought of Ansley. He was the one chance at a new beginning and she felt strangely close to him. She guessed it was because of the poetry. His words had resonated with her. Her life had been one of survival, of practicality and usefulness. Her protector had never been emotional. Art, and the range of emotions it inspired had seemed a great exposure. She had to be hidden, as did he, but she wanted to expose the better part of herself and felt like this new beginning would allow her to finally do exactly that. Like erasing a disastrous painting and activating anew, creation in the artistic sense, which is how she'd always thought of it. Ansley had created a world for himself inside of his words, which in a way, was what they were trying to do, but would he help? It hadn't gone well. What could she do to make him remember how beautiful the earth had been, how new and fresh?

A noise distracted her, it was a high-pitched mechanical whirl and so intense she felt her eardrums bending with the pressure. Her head swelled and she thought it might crack like a log in a fire. Also the heat, gnawing at her, hot needles down her ear canals. There was a clicking inside the whirl like the grinding of a gear.

It made her feel as though something were coming. There was doom in it and the omnipresent sense of a thing getting closer. She placed her hands over her ears in agony. Minutes as long as hours later the noise stopped. She lay there like a bell still vibrating after severe ringing and wished for her protector.

The leopard appeared with her telescope in its mouth. It dropped the telescope on her pillow and leapt up on the bed alert. A low growl began in the leopard's throat and with one paw he covered the telescope and with the other he swiped the air. Quickly Beatrice sat on the telescope. The leopard nodded and ever so gently brought his paw up to Beatrice's face. On its calloused pink pad lay a tiny dead mosquito.

"Is that what all the fuss is about? A mosquito?"

But the leopard's eyes shone with grave importance. He placed the mosquito inside a glass pitcher of water that sat beside the bed and put Beatrice's boot over the top it. The leopard sat as a guard at the foot of the bed. Beatrice lay down and watched the floating dead mosquito.

The leopard started purring and nuzzled Beatrice's ear, then jumped off the bed and stood guard near the door. She felt that she was in danger without knowing why. It reminded her of all the times she'd gone to sleep to the sounds of distant explosions. She rolled over on her back and held the telescope up in the air. It was tarnished bronze but she could just make out the letters of her name written on the side. There was a round cap with the same pattern as on the floor in the round wooden room, a cross of leaves, one of them was gold. She popped the cap open. The eye shined up at her. She held it up to the lantern and saw that it was a pattern composed of dots. Where had she seen that design before?

It reminded her of a dream she often had. She is in a room and the sun is like a shining peach behind the veil of the curtains. She opens the curtains, then removes the small crystal attached to a chain that she wears around her neck, and dangles it in the sunlight. Rainbows bounced off the walls in strange formations and that's it, that's the end of the dream.

She thought of Ansley who had never seen the sun. A hermit really, darker than that, a mole. We become what surrounds us. How does he see himself? She pictured a white candle shrouded by night. He was alone. A tiny white shine hidden in the city like a tuft of feather in a pool of oil. The world can be so savage, she thought, especially to the sensitive. Yet he had kept himself alive, which meant he had desire. She knew that wanting from life keeps us loving it.

Once she found a small mutant white bird and remembered how it had looked at her with a fear bordering on hatred. Its eyes were large and as rubbery as bouncy balls and it had one featherless fleshy wing nub that stuck out from its body like a hitchhiker's thumb. It had been blown to the ground in a storm.

God knows where it had been living or how it managed to survive without the use of both its wings. She kept it in a shoebox and listened to it scratch all night like a mouse. In the morning it was dead. She cried and said she should have let it sleep on the pillow. It might have scratched your eyes out, her protector had said. But it needed affection, she argued, love. No, he said, you can't tame wild creatures, it's too much of a risk. Ansley was a wild creature. They would have to take a risk with him and couldn't let him hate them enough to die.

She had a fantastic idea. She knew that Dex painted pictures of all the flowers he helped pollinate. She got up, grabbed the paints, and crept down the hallway.

When she reached the bottom of the stairs she could hear the gentle flow of conversation coming from behind a door. She recognized Dex's voice and stopped to listen.

21

"That went well didn't it?" Dex said with a tone of sarcasm.

"Oh stop it. God only knows what he's been through," said Marianne.

"And what about us? What about what we have been through? What about what we are going to go through? I mean we have to lose our lives," said Dex.

"He doesn't know any of that," said Marianne.

"Why don't you tell him? I certainly can't. Why don't you tell him what we are up against? And how important he is? If anyone can convince him it's you," said Dex.

"Just give him some time to adjust," she said.

"We don't have time!" Dex shouted.

Beatrice opened the door. They both looked up, surprised. Marianne and Dex were seated together at a table drinking glasses of water. Beatrice could see they'd eaten the French beans and grapes that she and Oren had left in a bowl.

"Sorry to interrupt," said Beatrice, looking around the kitchen. "This place is truly amazing. I was wondering if I could borrow some paints?"

This surprised Marianne. "Sit down," she said. "Join us."

Beatrice sat. "So," she said, "I have an idea but I need more paints. Do you have any that I could use?"

The walls looked like they'd been varnished or touched a thousand times. The floor was painted bright blue. There were mismatched glasses and plates on a wooden shelf. The room seemed to have been carved out like a bowl. Moths were in the center of the ceiling like a pendant light.

"Yes, but I need them to record plant and flower colors," said Dex, surprised. "Why? Do you paint?" Painting was the last thing on his mind.

"I did as a small child," said Beatrice.

"They are in the cupboard behind you," said Dex. "Help yourself."

Beatrice opened the door and took out the paint box. The cupboard was full of paints and brushes of all sizes.

"Where did you get all of these?" Beatrice asked.

"I entered a derelict classroom as a stray dog. I was sniffing around for food and found the art room unlocked. The more time passed the more I worried that I was forgetting the colors of things so I shifted into a human, grabbed as much as I could, and brought them here."

"He has a gallery," said Marianne, quietly.

"What? Here?"

"Yeah, here. Come on, we'll show you."

They opened another door. A small, ground-level one this time, that Beatrice had mistaken for a cupboard. Marianne crawled through, followed by Dex, then Beatrice. Once they were through the door they could stand up. Again the room looked as though it were an upside-down carved wooden bowl. She gasped with delight. The walls and ceiling were covered in trees, ferns, and flowers, and it was as though she'd stepped into a forest. She put her hand up to her face in awe.

"This is it! This is exactly what I wanted to do for Ansley!"

"What do you mean?" Marianne asked.

"I want to show him how beautiful a world can be, how pure, because he doesn't know, he's only seen darkness. It might make him see the importance of a new beginning, a chance. If it doesn't, then it will simply be a wonderful gift."

"Is that what you were going to use the paint for?"

"Yes I was going to paint his walls," said Beatrice.

"Decorate the walls and use these paintings as well," said Marianne.

"Are you serious? Really, you don't mind?" Beatrice jumped up and down with excitement.

"I mind," said Dex. "Those are my paintings and …" Marianne put her hand over Dex's mouth and silenced him.

"Of course we don't mind. It's a fantastic idea Beatrice," said Marianne.

"You go ahead and start painting and the moths will bring the gallery upstairs."

"Thank you," said Beatrice as she crawled through the doorway.

"It will never work," said Dex, after Beatrice had gone.

"It might," said Marianne. "You know how Ansley has a soft spot for kindness." Her voice was melancholy and she closed her eyes as if remembering.

"Why don't you go and help her if you find it so touching?" Dex mocked. "Make sure she doesn't waste all of my paint," he knew he sounded immature but didn't care.

He was sick of all this pandering towards Ansley. Didn't Marianne care that he had nearly been killed? She had often spoken of Ansley over the years and his supposed death had made a martyr out of him. Now that he's alive it's almost as though he holds the reverence of the resurrected and it was difficult for Dex to stomach.

He loved Marianne and wanted to begin a new life in the new world with her. As much as he had cared for his friendship with Ansley, there was no denying that his timely death had paved the way for Marianne and Dex's relationship. Among about a million other things like surviving and tracking down Emoli. Maybe things would have been different if they had been able to keep a hold of the baby, but Jude had intercepted that plan.

He tried not to blame Marianne, but if she would have just kept the pearl herself they might be living the good life by now, instead of waiting for Ansley to sweep in and save the day. He took a deep breath and fingered the coin in his pocket. Try to be realistic, reasonable, he chastised himself, and above all else, stay focused. Ansley was purely a means to an end. He had her love because he had her history, beside there was little chance that Ansley would survive the phosforest anyway. And that's assuming he'd help them in the first place. He'd just have to be patient and control his temper, he thought, as he flicked the coin in the air and caught it.

Ah ha, thought Nelly, as she followed him up the stairs.

***

Very carefully Beatrice opened the door to Ansley's room. He, too, had fallen asleep in his clothes on the bed. It had been a long night. For a moment she looked at him. He was so unique. His skin was the color of a pale shell. He was not outwardly attractive, but he was introspective and brave, which blended its own glow. A disfigured face shrouded by a white veil. He was softly snoring. Good. That way she'll know if he wakes or not. The moths entered soundlessly with the paintings. A few broke away and gently plugged his ears and blindfolded his eyes.

She tiptoed to the wall. I'll have to be quick, she thought, opening the tubes of paint. She'd paint a sun, ground, and stems, she thought, as the moths suspended paintings over the ceiling and along the walls. Each one was illuminated by a moth's abdomen like a candlelit gallery. It was already stunning. She smiled to herself, crossed her heart, and hoped it worked.

22

In the morning they had breakfast on a large deck that swept around the circumference of the tree. All around them fanned moth wings draped like curtains through which the sun shone and cast a pinkish sheen over everything, yet it was dark enough for Ansley. It was like being inside a chapel with stained-glass windows. On the table were various mismatched plates, cutlery, and bowls of fruit. Oren and Beatrice were talking intensely when Ansley approached.

"Good morning," said Oren. "Take a seat," but Ansley ignored him and walked straight to Beatrice.

"Was it you?" Ansley asked her.

"Yes. Do you mind?" Beatrice knew he was referring to the paintings.

"Mind? Are you kidding? It's the single nicest thing anyone has ever done for me, ever. I don't know how to thank you."

He had been astounded when he woke up. He had never opened his morning eyes to a flower before, let alone a whole world of them. The moths had held the paintings up so that they hovered and hummed with life.

"It wasn't only me. Those paintings belong to Dex. He said I could borrow them," said Beatrice. Ansley looked at her with surprise and sat down.

"What are you two talking about?" said Oren.

"I created a daytime scene on Ansley's wall," Beatrice explained.

"What, like the sun and things?" Beatrice nodded yes. "That was nice of you," said Oren.

"I felt bad about reading your poems yesterday Ansley," she said. "I'm still really sorry about that."

"Was that only yesterday? It seems like weeks ago. And, believe me, you have been well and truly forgiven," said Ansley.

"There was also another reason," said Beatrice, and chose her words with care. "I wanted to show you how beautiful the new planet could be, just in case, you know, you wanted to help us," she said quietly, but with direct eye contact.

Ansley stared at her, searching. "Will it really look like that?"

"Oren and I are carrying all of those seeds, so if we make it there, then, yes, it will," she said, and Oren nodded.

Ansley fell silent. He picked up an orange and peeled it, thinking.

Dex barged through the door and placed a dish of flatbread and strawberries down on the table. The table was made of polished bark and the chairs were branches of the tree that had twisted around and held themselves under the table as seats.

Ansley stared at the strawberries, it had been years since he had a strawberry. Dex noticed.

"Have the first one," he said, handing him a plate. "A peace offering."

"Thank you," said Ansley, as he took a strawberry.

"I'm sorry about yesterday," Dex said, and held his hand out towards Ansley. "It was a shock for all of us, most of all you," he knew that he had to make amends with Ansley if he was to keep Marianne. "Maybe we could start over?"

Ansley looked at him, then took his hand and reluctantly shook it.

"I'm shocked you are standing here in front of me," said Dex. "All this time we thought you were dead."

"And yet I survived," Ansley said sarcastically.

"But how?" Dex didn't rise to the sarcasm.

"On rat, basically."

"And beetle it seems," Marianne walked into the room.

"Only for a treat," he thought of Nelly and his face relaxed into a smile.

"Ansley we had no idea," said Marianne.

"How could you? You've been holed up in the lap of luxury eating strawberries," he said.

"I know it looks like that, but we have had struggles as well," Marianne said, and reached out to touch his arm. He let her. He felt tired. "We would have come for you earlier, but we only just found out. This strange little beetle told us there was a ghost boy in London and we just knew it was you, didn't we Dex?"

"Yep and now you're here. It's like it's all falling into place now," said Dex, with a conviction that he didn't feel.

But what could he have done? He couldn't keep quiet about the beetle because the fate of the new world rested on Ansley's condition.

"What's falling into place? Your master plan? Kill me off for a year to, I suspect, your great advantage and summon me when I'm needed like some crappy zombie? Well done, Dr. Dex."

Nelly piped in. "That's it! Give him hell!"

"Hush Nelly," Ansley said.

"Nelly?" Dex asked.

"I ate her beetle and now she visits me," said Ansley.

The rest of them exchanged glances and watched him apprehensively. Ansley saw the uneasy look on their faces. He stopped eating.

"What? You think it's perfectly reasonable to be standing in the middle of an invisible tree with two shape-shifters and God knows what you are," he waved at Beatrice and Oren, "but you start to worry about my sanity when I tell you I can see and hear the ghost of the corpse the carrion beetle I ate was feeding on? Suddenly that's weird in the midst of all of this? Something is seriously wrong with you people," said Ansley, taking another bite of flatbread.

"They haven't even told you why you're here," said Nelly, sitting on Oren's lap and blowing on his neck. He shivered from the cold, but couldn't see her at all.

"You haven't even told me why I'm here," said Ansley, and Nelly nodded.

"You're right," said Marianne. "And that's the main point. We just thought you were alone and are a little shocked to discover you have a tag along," she said.

"Tag along?! I am no tag along," Nelly said, and air punched Marianne, making her blink. Moths fluttered out of her hair and up into the rafters.

"Nelly is not a tag along. She is free to come and go as she pleases. She's usually touring and is gone for months," Ansley said.

"Touring?" Beatrice asked.

"She's an actress," said Ansley and Beatrice nodded as if that explained everything. The rest of them just looked at one another with eyebrows raised, Marianne changed the subject.

"After we found your ring, everything changed," she said.

23

Marianne described what had happened. She described how they'd given the pearl to Emoli to keep it safe. "Remember the cove and the tower of chalk?"

"As if I'd ever forget it," he whispered, and Beatrice noticed Dex's jaw clench.

"What cove?" Dex asked.

"The one where the scale entered my hand," Marianne said impatiently to Dex, and then turned back to Ansley. "Turns out that scale was one of Jude's tracking devices. He found us and he stole Emoli and now we need to rescue him."

"What makes you sure that Emoli isn't dead?" Ansley asked.

"He has the pearl inside of him, protected by his water," said Marianne slowly. "So he's safe."

"Safe until Jude discovers how to remove the pearl," Dex interrupted.

"Why don't we just steal him back?" Ansley asked.

"It's not as simple as that. He is protected by Jude's swamp lair," said Dex.

"I thought you said he hated water?"

"Pure water," said Dex.

"The moths have discovered that there is a way to destroy Jude once and for all," said Marianne. "We can destroy him and take back Emoli at the same time."

"Great. How? Chop his head off?" Ansley said.

"Sadly, no. You must pierce his heart with a vaccine," said Marianne.

"A vaccine of what?" Ansley said.

"Pure oxygen," said Marianne, and Ansley could feel that she was stalling. "When I say pure I mean, high potency. Jude is a silicon creature and if we blast him with oxygen he will explode."

"Right, so how do we get it?"

"There is only one place that has the strength level that we need. It grows on a tree in the form of a fruit that friends of Dex's parents were working on years ago. The fruit looks like a little lung. It was created to offer oxygen to people living in high pollution zones," she said.

"Why do I feel like there is a catch here?"

"Because there is. This is where you come into the equation Ansley. The plasmid tree replicates the lungs we need but it only grows in the phosforest."

"The phosforest? Don't they make sport of tenderizing enemies?" Ansley asked.

"You are the only mammal who can enter the phosforest without being eaten," Marianne was calm.

"Eaten by what?" Beatrice asked, alarmed.

"The plants. The forests destroy a mammal's ability to reproduce and so, as the plant species have mutated, they've been given the ability to smell mammalian reproductive organs. And they tend to eat enemies," Dex said.

"So why can he enter without becoming mincemeat?" Oren said.

"Because he doesn't have a single sweat gland. He has no scent whatsoever. Isn't that incredible?" Marianne took him by the shoulders. "I'm sure the pearl knew that when you swallowed its waters, remember? Dex was right when he said that your condition was needed. It didn't heal you because you're our miracle Ansley."

24

"She's right," said Dex. "We can't do this without you. If we have the fruit we can extract its seeds and mix them with a vaccine I have been concocting. Since the seed contains such a high potency of oxygen, if we mix it with a replicon then we can explode him into sand and spread his particles."

"Repliwhat?" Oren said.

"Replicons are molecules that can transfer certain genetic elements through a host. Dex is a wiz at altering seeds and cross germination. Come on, let's go to the obsidian room and explain it in greater detail."

"What is the obsidian room?" Beatrice said.

"It's where we keep the vaccine. It's like a safe," said Dex.

"So do you even know where Emoli is?" said Beatrice.

"We don't know much about it except that he's kept in Jude's infected swamp. We guess that Jude is trying to corrupt his water so that he can enter him and take the pearl."

"How did you find that out?"

"Martin told us. When the cherubs attacked the used car lot Martin captured one and persuaded it to speak. But as soon as we activate Emoli the green smoke you see through your telescopes should tell you where he's hidden," said Dex. "But we can't activate him without being ready. We have one chance. The smoke signal only lasts for twenty-four hours.

So what about it Ansley? I know it's a lot to ask, but are you willing to help us? You would be putting your life at risk."

"Ansley you are the only one that can do it, please, otherwise, well, humanity is lost," Marianne said, stepped forward, and touched his arm. He flicked her hand away.

"Excuse me? Haven't you noticed? Humanity was lost a long time ago. It's gone, poof, vanished! I haven't seen a living ounce of it since I left Rye," said Ansley.

"This is a different meaning to humanity. This is humanity's second chance."

"What makes you think we even deserve a second chance? We made such a cock up of the first! Why don't you just let us die out and give the next species a chance?"

"What are you talking about! We *are* the next species, look at us – not a 'normal' human in the group. This is it! We are it!" Marianne shouted.

"No. Not 'we' Marianne, you. You are the next species. Not me. I'm just the ghostly minion who has to risk my life so that yours may continue in, I don't know, some kind of utopia, happily ever after while I get to go back to living in a lock up, eating rats with some dead drama queen," he said.

 "Ansley … ," Marianne reached for him.

"Don't. Just don't touch me.

"Ansley please stop being so angry. We went back for you. I've said it a million times and each time it's true, if we'd have known that you were alive we would have come for you before …"

"Before I became useful to you?" Ansley cut her off.

"Well, yes, but that's not what I mean," she said.

"Isn't it?" Ansley said. "Is there any proof? I mean, what if we're doing this for nothing? It's a *pearl* Marianne, a *pearl*. How in the hell will it become a new planet? What do you even know about it anyway?"

It all seemed so far-fetched. He'd thought about the pearl many times over the last year and each time he couldn't even imagine how it could seed a planet.

"I thought you might ask that question. Let me show you something," Marianne said, pulling a moth from her ear and releasing it into Ansley's ear.

It fluttered against his mind like wind against a fire and he lit up. He saw everything. A world. The earth was black and plentiful, yet there were no plants, trees, nothing but lush soil and water, magnificently blue water, crystal bright seas that held animals inside their white-capped waves. Wave horses, wave zebra, and elephants just perched and waiting to emerge. He saw a leopard leap and spray across the wave only to dissolve onto the sand. The clouds were animal shapes. A misty lion, a squirrel, all perched on the edge and ready to jump into form. All trapped. Animals were everywhere, in the swirls of sand, inside the clumps of mud, and on breezes. They stood on four rings of glittering minerals that circled the planet waiting to materialize. Their faces were solemn. He had uncapped their sky. It seemed to offer change and every so often one would look at him then beat frantically against his form before falling back into the wind, exhausted. Time was running out.

It flew out of his mind and into Marianne's hair. Ansley sat speechless for a moment.

"If I get the seeds will I be able to live there as well?"

"I'm not sure. None of us are sure of the new forms we'll take. There is something else you should know. We offer the elements. The Growers carry the seeds. Meaning, to activate the new world we will have to explode," said Marianne, and they all sat in reverence while Ansley digested this information.

"Explode?" Ansley whispered.

"We'll come back. Think of it as scattering to reorganize. But how that will work is uncertain, so you see, we are not without our own sacrifice," she said.

"Or fears," said Beatrice.

"Exactly," said Marianne. "But we have to believe."

"How do you know all of this?" Ansley asked.

"She explained some things, yes, but remember the wings I showed you?" Marianne asked as she stepped inside the pentagram. "The burns weren't just wings. One they'd healed we saw that they were words," she said, and lowered the straps of her dress to reveal her back. A large tree began at the base of her spine and branched up past her neck line and around the curve of her shoulders. The moths organized into lanterns and hung above the tree. The tattoo was composed entirely of words. Scripture, thought Ansley, and he imagined Dex reading it. Marianne turned and saw his face.

"Martin was the first to read my instructions," she said. "They had been preparing for this, for all of us."

25

“Martin?” Ansley asked. “The Martin we met?” He couldn’t bring himself to look at Dex. He remembered that windblown night as the last in their friendship.

“The same one,” said Dex. “After we lost Emoli, Martin took us here. The tree was ready. She explained the Growers and their guardians. It was all a part of the Original Seed’s prophecy and Martin was able to understand Marianne’s instructions, at least some of it.”

“There are the stories that you’ve been told,” Marianne nodded to the Growers. “You hold the seeds and Martin knew this, so prepared this tree for initiation and finally, activation. But how to begin was another question,” she hesitated. “It was difficult after Emoli was taken. I could feel the pearl dying and Emoli along with it. I can’t describe the guilt, the despair I felt,” she turned to Ansley. “You, out of everyone, know how important the pearl was to me. Imagine my losing it, losing a child …” she trailed off.

Ansley thought of her on the night of the chalk stack. How her face had glowed when she showed him the pearl as though she had a lit bulb cupped inside her hands. And her hair, wind whipped into strands as thick as seaweed. She believed her future was inside of that pearl, her destiny, it was how she justified the cruelty around her. He had understood this because he had felt the same thing when he looked at her. He crushed that image inside of his mind and saw that she, too, had suffered, perhaps more than him because he had already known what it was like to live without hope. She had not. For him, losing hope had felt tragically familiar. He softened.

"Tell us," he said. "What changed you? Healed you?"

She could hear the concern in his voice and this lightened her, lightened the room. "Martin helped me," she said. "And Dex, of course, but I slept for a long time and while I was sleeping I had the same remarkable dream."

26

She was standing at the edge of a foaming sea. She plunged through the foam and entered the deep water. Beneath her she saw silver tree roots like feet poking out from underneath a curtain. They seemed inhumanly real. How odd, she thought. She rose to the surface for a breath and was confronted with a wall of water. A giant wave of black water. It was a door. She could see the watery keyhole and immediately swam through it, twisting her body like a golden key. The other side was not a sea at all, but a forest, shimmering as if covered by frost. The trees were seemingly enclosed with a molten glass that was hardened white. As if each tree had been dipped in hot almond bark. It made her mouth water. She swam, in the air this time, not the water, above the tops of trees all reaching for her with endless arms. White metal fingers. A forest of dead coral. They were faceless.

She woke up. Being in the forest reminded her of the minds she'd entered. The first mind she had been able to enter was Jude's and that was terrifying. She spent her nights relentlessly searching for Emoli or his captors. She entered as many sleeping minds as she could, looking for clues. She flew in through an ear and transformed into an electrical impulse new world. Over the years she envisaged her hunt as a long, wire-thin root weaving through minds in search of the perfect vein of water. Mostly she'd found regret and loneliness, like stamping hooves to the spirit, or fear: that unforgettable echo that coiled around the mind like a white snake. Some nights the echo rang so loud in her that she felt herself a bell and her spinal cord the rope that wickedness yanked. She tingled with the ruin of it. The waste. And then, always when she needed it most, just like a fleet of buses, a night of beautiful minds. She'd sit on their brains and watch their synapses spark like a brilliant fireworks show. Bright fish flicking through a maze of white. It was such a welcome sight, like the face of the one you love in a featureless crowd. Each night, her wings flew and flew, entered spaces, purple against the white, against midnight, blue. The spaces like the space around a planet and prickling with largesse, that particular stir of possibility, that calm shrill. It was a time in her life when the nights were twice as long as days. And empty, but nothing like empty, a tundra with life underneath.

It was how she found Oren, although she wasn't sure of his importance in the beginning, not until her dream changed.

Oren was sleeping. Marianne waited motionless against the floral wallpaper in perfect camouflage and took a moment to reflect. She had entered so many tonight, an infant even, with tight fists and butternut skin. It had stopped crying as she flew around it, even laughed a little as she flew down its throat as if it were ticklish, and for a moment, Marianne wondered if this child was a clue, but there was no explosion when she entered the chest's chamber. Just the rhythmic swooshing of the heart and the lungs branching out like a sleeping miniature jungle. She left the child peaceful, wide-eyed, and staring at the ceiling.

She looked at the boy on the bed. His breath had small sounds in it and she wondered what they meant. He was the evening's last. Her wings could not take another try. Already they were too wet with human mucus as if she'd flown ground level through the dew. Human dew is quite a nice way to describe spit. She tried not to think about the drawbacks. She has a mission never mind the means, she says to herself, and looks out the window into the emerging violet world. Soon she will fly out into a damp dawn after another night of searching and the bodies will float like vignettes through her memory, rearranging the rooms she's entered. She'll savor the ones that tasted sweet with possibility and drop the sour through the air like dislodging feathers. It kept her optimistic. It kept her seeking. She turned to the man and shifted like a secret into his mouth where she was met with the sun before it exploded. They exploded, his chest like a burst pillow of stars, each a burning imprint of life, gold dust. He knew nothing of that spleen-splitting moment. His head like some heavy planet lay shadowed on the pillow while she watched his atoms reform and fizzle through the air like golden embroidery. He was full of seeds. She sat on the bedpost and watched him sleep, round, regal, and brown like some earthly idol. Her love was immediate.

And a thought came to her that felt wild and absolute. She needed to enter Martin. She needed to know the secrets Martin held.

27

The inside of Martin's brain felt familiar, normal, the white forest reminded her of all the time she'd spent in the brain. Finding Oren was like watching a tulip open in the spring and she felt justified for the time she'd spent wintering. The trees were the same crystallized white and faceless, spiritless. Except one. The scripture tree. She had never seen it before. It was huge and rose out of the darkness, rose beyond the grabbing and touched the sun. It was the only tree that was not frozen. It had rich brown bark and bright green leaves. It was covered with scripture, like small, cursive, and golden embroidered lettering. It seemed to hear her coming. It turned and reached out a limb in her direction and from its bough, apples dangled like ruby earrings. It seemed full of sun. She could hear it thriving like a hive of gold. A branch contorted into the shape of her face. Another branch became the shape of an unknown hand that gently picked two apples off neighboring branches and pressed one into each of her eyes.

Suddenly the white forest was alive. She saw shadows darting all around her and behind trees as quick as squirrels. They looked like pudgy little people. There was a tinkling music but it was distant and sad like an echo through a tunnel.

"Don't worry, they are harmless. They are cherubs left over from the Fall," said a raspy voice behind her. She turned and saw nothing.

"Down here," he said, and started coughing and sputtering. Eventually he lit a cigarette. "That's better," he said, and smiled at Marianne who stared at him with equal amounts of disgust and disbelief.

"Who are you?"

"Hhhhhhh. The eternal question. I am many. I am thousands of years old. The older you get the more complicated it becomes, believe me. I am someone that you can believe," he said. "Hear that?"

"The music?"

"Yes, the music. It's coming from another world," he said.

"What world?"

"The world you'll find with the white seed," he said, blowing out cigarette smoke. Marianne thought his skin was like a plucked chicken.

"The white seed? You mean the pearl?"

"Is that what you call it? It has many names, just as the scripture tree has many names, but only one purpose, one power."

The shadows bounced from white tree to white tree laughing little tinkling laughs. She couldn't make out the meaning of their whispers.

"How is that possible?"

"How everything is possible of course, through miracle."

"What power is that?"

The old cherub started coughing. Marianne watched its rolls of dimply fat shake and its stretched out belly button wobble. He was hacking away and eventually brought up a brownish green glob of phlegm, which he spat next to Marianne's foot. A bit splattered on to her toes. He looked up at her and smiled a wide disgusting smile. He had three rolls of fat under his chin and dimples in his cheeks the size of slashes. His teeth were green and speckled with black from the nicotine. Marianne turned away in revulsion.

"Look again Marianne," he said, his voice changing towards the end of the sentence getting higher, lighter.

When she turned to look again the old cherub had changed into a beautiful, ethereal voluptuous woman. She had flaxen knee-length hair that covered her bottom and her breasts. In her eyes there was a fierce wisdom.

"Be sure to always look again before you decide what it is you are seeing. Here, take these," she said, and touched Marianne's wings.

"What are they?"

"Instructions. Don't you know?"

"No I don't," she was feeling frustrated.

"Everything you need to inhabit your world is already inside of you. Inside of all of you. Find the others and unlock yourselves," she said, as her body began to pull apart like taffy until it had become wisps of cloud.

The cloud burst into rain. Big fat metallic drops of rain shot into Marianne's skin with the intention of arrows. She began to convulse. Her arms and legs spread and pulsed with electricity. It was as though someone was burning her back. Flames shot from behind her and she could smell burnt flesh.

"Am I dying?!"

"Only the worst in you," said the woman's voice.

"But why? Why me?"

"You who shift between realms must find the cultivators. They are known to us as the Growers and we have sent four guardians from the animal kingdom to protect them. The Growers share a heart with their animal guardians. That's what I can tell you."

The cloud stopped raining. She could hear the woman laughing. It was not a mean laugh. The cloud rose above the scripture tree. The tree's branches wiggled like tickling fingers and the laughter increased. All around her shadows skipped and the murmured sound of many excited voices softly pinged against the trees. She saw something. A single feather was floating down through the boughs of the scripture tree. It was white with a blue iridescent hue. It shimmered and when it landed on the ground everything went completely silent. It was as though someone had stopped a record.

That's when the serpent came. He came like a scream through the silent wood. At first she thought he was a ball of fire spat from the clouds. A giant flaming arrow, she thought, but then she saw his eyes. They blazed with a terrible greed. His body was one long phosphorescent muscle that drilled through the sky. He was a serpent and he was aiming right at her. He laughed a malicious, splintered-tooth laugh and opened his mouth wide, when abruptly, inches in front of her face, he stopped. Well, he didn't so much stop as splat, as if he'd hit a wall, an invisible wall between Marianne and the serpent. She was too startled to be scared.

"It's you. Why are you here? What exactly *are* you?"

"The guardian Jude. I am Jude," he said, licking the bump on his head with his long forked tongue. He, too, seemed completely stunned and began to shout while pounding his tail against the ground in anger.

But Marianne wasn't listening. She picked the feather up and it lifted her off the ground. She was flying again and when she looked down at Jude he seemed small and helpless. Like the snakes she'd seen wiggling under her father's boot. In her mind, she took out her pocketknife and cut his head off.

"Martin didn't wake up. But I was awake. I was more awake than I'd ever been and my back fiercely itched. I shifted back into human form and scratched all of the scabs off. I used my fingernails and a stick. It felt like I could scratch out of myself, like I could scratch my skin off. It took hours and when I'd finished I found words. Instructions," she said, and stepped into the pentagram and lowered the straps of her dress.

28

The wings were a part of the foliage now and a huge tree spread across her back. The trunk of the tree was Marianne's spine and on either side were branches that read:

To get there one must dig   Find it written like a map

in peaceful stealth   inside a human bulb.

Deep

in frost

the world

waits

for her

inhibitors.

"Once we are all inside the helix, the Growers will unlock and the world will open to the chosen," said Marianne.

"Where is the helix?" asked Beatrice.

"Look up," said Marianne.

Sure enough it looked as though a drill had tunneled through the tree and there was a corkscrew design carved into the middle of the trunk. At the bottom was the circle with their name on it.

"Emoli is the final Grower as he's swallowed the Original Seed," said Marianne. "The power inside of me is stronger now and my connection with the pearl has never ceased. If I can feel it dying then Jude must be able to see the light in Emoli diminishing. He knows that time is running out. Soon the seed won't propagate. Soon it will deteriorate. Jude knows this. But having a new world at your disposal is one thing, knowing how to use it is quite another. And *we* know how to use it, not Jude, us," Marianne said to Ansley.

For as long as she could remember she often felt as though she were waiting for a particular destiny to reveal itself, although she did not yet know what that might mean, she knew that the pearl was the crux from which that destiny would unravel. She was similar to the way the pearl had been inside the clam. She felt locked inside the constraints of the world and the irritability she suffered was her own scratching destiny. On those unquiet days, and there were many, she thought of seeds. She thought of their small, dark souls and remembered that a seed could lay waiting for thirty years or more before the sun burst through and summoned it to grow. It gave her hope. Her mind, she thought, was like a lock, like this dark chamber around a sleeping heart and she, too, was rare and encased in a coating as thick as a bird's beak. She would gladly break through herself. Yes. Just like a seed, just like the tiny green foot cares not at all if it bruises, even snaps, as it courageously pushes its way to freedom. Why if nature can break through its tomb and grow, then surely a mind, a thing of matter, for who are we to question nature? Her body, after all, had broken through its form, and it seemed as though the rest of her was waiting to follow.

But how could she explain this to Ansley, to everyone? How could she tell them that she felt as though she wasn't fully formed? When looking at him was a fist in the chest, when she was leading them all into a world uncharted, when the only known was danger. She couldn't.

"We just need you to help us find the vaccine," was all she could say, but strung between those words was the thread of her existence.

And Ansley felt it. He felt her snapping like something lost in the wind, the sound of being at the mercy of another.

"Okay," Ansley said, and took Marianne's hand. "For you."

"Thank you," said Marianne, and they stared at one another. Moths fluttered in and out of their gaze. "Thank you."

"Anyway," Dex said, breaking the spell. "I'm sure you'll be fine. We are pretty certain that Jude doesn't know the purpose of our Growers."

"I'm not so sure about that," said Beatrice. "Something strange happened last night." They all turned towards her as she took the mosquito out of her pocket.

"I heard a sound, a large whirling noise, but there was something mechanical about it, I can't put my finger on it. I know I've heard it before. Anyway it came closer and closer then it stopped. My leopard protector arrived and caught this mosquito. He trapped it in the water pitcher and didn't leave my side until morning."

"It might be a helifly," Dex said. "Put it in this," he reached into the deep pocket of his dressing gown and pulling out a Petri dish with a lid. "Let's take him in to the kitchen and have a look."

29

Dex viewed the fly through his microscope and consulted a notebook of hand-drawn creatures that he'd taken from a cupboard.

"That's a spy all right," said Dex, tapping the drawing with his finger and picking up the tweezers. "A young one. If you look here you'll see an extra antenna. Plus it's much bigger than your average fly and there is this," he said, pinching the abdomen with his tweezers and releasing a hornet-sized stinger. "A weapon with a punch."

"Where did you get that book?" Beatrice asked.

"Martin. She drew all of the things we needed to be careful of."

"Is it something you could shift into?" Marianne asked.

Dex picked up the helifly and stroked its back. A dark fatigue came over him and he could feel himself weakening.

"Yes. I could shift, but I don't think it's wise. I might fall under his command."

"Can you get any information from him?" asked Beatrice.

"We'll see. Come with me, I want to show you something as well as put him somewhere safe."

They followed Dex around the decking to the other side of the tree where he pointed to a small perfectly smooth and flat obsidian arrowhead dangling from a tree branch by a bit of spider's web. Beatrice looked up and saw an enormous corn spider quietly spinning a web the size of a large tablecloth. Dex held the arrowhead to his eye and immediately the arrow took flight and plunged seamlessly into the stomachs of Beatrice, Ansley, and Oren and out again. It took their breath away.

"It's just checking your authenticity, sorry," Dex explained.

The obsidian arrowhead stood upright in front of Dex and began to grow until it was a six-by-six-foot triangle that Dex stepped through indicating for them to follow. They looked at one another. Oren nudged his head to Beatrice. You first. Beatrice stepped through and entered an obsidian hallway. It was like walking through a cool black sea or walking on air through the black sky.

"So what would have happened if the arrowhead had found us unsuitable?" Beatrice asked.

"You saw the giant webs overhead right?"

"Yeah."

"They would have dropped them on you, rolled you until you suffocated, and then sucked your liquids out."

"That's quite extreme," said Oren.

"Yes, isn't nature amazing?" Dex said.

Ahead of him was Marianne. She was holding something that glistened like the pearl. It was a small plant looking very much like a stalagmite covered with radiant minuscule barnacles.

"How wonderful, look, it's the color of you," Beatrice said to Ansley.

"So it is," said Marianne. She took a small vial from her pocket and delicately snapped off a few of the petals from the vaccine plant. She placed the petals in the vial and turned to Ansley.

"Here, squeeze the plasmid fruit's juice into the vial and shake it up. *Voilà*, a complete vaccine. These are for you," she said, as she turned to Beatrice. She handed her two obsidian arrowheads.

"Just throw the arrowhead into the air and shout the name of the thing you want it to pierce and destroy. It will only take orders from you."

"Will it destroy Jude?" Beatrice asked.

"Yes, if it doesn't destroy him entirely, it will certainly weaken him enough for you to pierce him with the vaccine," said Marianne.

"Why couldn't we strap the vaccine to the arrow and tell it to pierce his heart?" said Beatrice.

"That's an excellent idea," said Dex.

"How did you find the vaccine anyway?" said Oren.

"Dex found her in a small stream trickling through a cave at the bottom of a volcano. He had to turn himself into a bat. Touch its leaves," she held the plant up to Beatrice.

Beatrice felt the barnacles and realized they weren't hard at all but in fact very soft and velvety like a lamb's ears.

"How did you know where to find it?" Oren asked Dex.

"I didn't. It was a total fluke. I was collecting around the mouth of the volcano, inactive of course, hence my bat form, and decided to take a fly around. I had Marianne in my mind and wanted to show her the sights. I kept hearing water. My human ears would never have been able to detect such a small hidden stream but as a bat I was supersonic. I flew towards the sound and found this beauty."

"Did you know it was the vaccine?"

"No. But I knew," said Marianne. "I knew right away. I was reborn with it imprinted on my mind. I didn't know it would be so small though. I guess things feel towering when they seem unobtainable."

"Yeah like finding Emoli feels to me at the moment," Oren said.

"Let's concentrate on one thing at a time, first Valentine," said Beatrice.

"Good plan. Okay, first Valentine."

"First phosforest," said Ansley, and they each looked at him admiringly.

"That's right," said Dex. "I have something to help you. Heliflies patrol the phosforest and you'll need protection."

"I don't need anything from you," said Ansley.

"Ansley," said Marianne. "These flies are infantry. They're mini-soldiers for Jude and the flies in the phosforest, well, they test your blood," she explained.

"My what?!"

"Your blood. I know it's a bit of a pain."

"It's more than a pain!"

"Yes, well, it's unavoidable I'm afraid. But here, take this needle, it doesn't look like much but it just might save you. The helifly will rear back after it has found the perfect place for its taste test, you use that time to prick its chosen spot and a blister will balloon with blood. Not the blood of a mammal of course, you see, it's testing you to see if you are a mammal. Once it realizes you are an insect it will just fly away. Do you understand?"

"Yeah, I understand, this whole trip is a death wish. What is this anyway?" he said, looking down at the needle.

"It's a wasp's tail. Martin magicked it up, she's just brilliant in the kitchen. Look Ansley, we'd never ask this of you if it wasn't completely necessary," said Marianne.

"Yes but that doesn't make it any less daunting," said Beatrice.

They looked at the plant, lost in their own thoughts.

"Listen, how about we activate Valentine together? Come on, it will be fun," said Dex.

They walked back to the main room. The opals were lit and glowing. Dex knelt beside the cross on the floor and used his finger to trace the name written in one of the four leaves. The leaf was turning golden. Two leaves were already bright gold and one remained a dark green.

"Your name is written on this one," Ansley told Beatrice. He was standing next to one of the golden leaves.

"And mine is written on this one, look," said Oren in excitement.

"The leaf turns gold when you are stimulated," Dex looked up from his work.

"When will you stimulate Emoli?" Beatrice asked.

"There should only be twenty-four hours between each leaf, which means you only have one day."

"And two nights if we leave now," said Ansley.

"Yes, of course, two nights. It would be wise to leave tonight. Ansley can only travel that way, and Beatrice, Oren, you two could really cover some ground. Valentine should be easy to fetch. Her leaf points east, so walk towards the east and you should begin to see her green smoke signal."

"Emoli's leaf, the dark green is pointing south. Should I just start walking south after I've collected the plasmid fruit?" said Ansley.

"Yes," said Marianne. "I will command the moths to wait at the southern edge of the phosforest and lead you to the others. I will be with them."

Dex was startled. "Marianne you can't. You know it's too risky to leave the tree," he said.

"I can look after myself Dex, don't worry. The moths will protect me."

"You'll be too vulnerable Marianne." He was standing beside her now and grabbed her arm.

"Dex, I know what I'm doing!" She pushed his hand away.

"I know what you're doing too! You are risking yourself because you feel some debt to him," he pointed at Ansley. "You are the initiator Marianne. The planet can't form without you. Just drop the guilt you feel. It was not your fault okay?! We went back for him. If anyone is to blame, it's me. I pushed him away in the first place. I'll go with the moths. I'll risk it but not you," he reached for her and she let him hold her. "It doesn't matter if I die, but you, you are needed."

"You are needed too," she said quietly. "I need you," she broke away from him and turned towards Ansley. "And you, so please can we put aside our differences."

Dex and Ansley nodded in begrudging agreement, which was better than nothing, yet a long way from resolved. She sensed that she couldn't leave them alone without consequence and as much as it pained her to think it, she didn't trust either one to focus without letting their grudges overrule. The pygmy blue moth was the size of a fingernail and the weight of a feather. It could easily travel undetected on Dex.

"So it's settled then. Head south Ansley. Dex and the moths will meet you there. As for Oren and Beatrice," she turned around and found Oren eating strawberries he'd pulled from his stomach. Beatrice was missing.

"Where is Beatrice?" Marianne asked.

Oren hadn't been paying attention. "I don't know. You guys were talking and she went upstairs. I figured she had to go to the toilet or something and I didn't want to interrupt. Strawberry?" He handed her one and she looked at him with impatience.

"Beatrice?!" Marianne called up the stairs.

"Coming!" Beatrice came bouncing down the stairs and everyone gasped.

30

She had chopped off her hair and shaved her head. The skin across her head was as tight and soft as a baseball. She walked up to Ansley and handed him a thick black braid tied with leather bands at either end so that it was a rope the length of an arm. He looked at her in disbelief.

"For luck," she said, and winked at him.

"Oh my God. I don't know what to say, thank you. I can't believe you did this," he took the braid and ran his hand up and down it. It was so silky and beautiful.

"Oh Beatrice," Marianne said, touched her shining scalp. "I'm speechless."

"We all are," said Oren.

"It's not that big of a deal. Besides I don't know why I didn't do it ages ago. I feel so much lighter now," she gave Ansley a huge hug. "I wanted you to have something human, you know, to take with you."

Ansley looked at Beatrice with transformed faith. It was as simple as that. Over the last twenty-four hours she had consistently managed to renew him with unexpected gestures of incredible kindness. For the first time he didn't see the girl in her but a glimmer of the woman. This girl will become magnificent, he thought, she already is.

"Thank you for this gift," he said. "I am honored to be fulfilling this task with a part of you beside me," and stuck his arm out for Beatrice to take. "Let's go," he said, as she linked her arm around his. "Let's get this done."

***

The three of them stood at the foot of the tree and faced the field beyond in silence. Each was reluctant to move, to place the future in motion like starting an uncontrollable car. Beatrice held her telescope up and saw a distant green smoke had begun to rise in the air like a signal. She turned to Ansley and Oren and broke the silent spell.

"Looks like we are going this way," she said, and pointed in the opposite direction of the phosforest. "How will you do it?" She looked at Ansley.

"I'm not sure. I guess I'll just do what I always do and listen to the small voice inside me, not the loud arrogant one. The small one is usually right. But apart from that I have no idea," said Ansley.

Oren stuck out his hand and Ansley shook it. "Good luck," he said.

"Thank you, I think I'll need it. Good luck to you too," Ansley said, and turned to Beatrice. Her scalp was like a moon against the sky.

"And thank you, for everything, the painting and, I really never thought I'd be saying this, but thank you for your hair. I wanted to give you something as well."

He reached into his pocket and produced his notebook of poems. He ripped he last few blank pages off and handed the rest to Beatrice.

"It's all I have to offer. Read them all and if you hate them, please lie to me."

"I will," she smiled.

"Thank you."

"I mean I will read them all and I know I'll love them," she said, and for a moment they stared at one another, then hugged.

"Goodbye," she said.

"Not goodbye. It's see you soon," he told her.

"Yes. You're right. See you soon, bald as the moon," she laughed and ran to catch up with Oren who was already walking towards the green smoke.

"I hope," he said, as he touched her braid. It was in his coat pocket like a breastplate. He turned to face the phosforest. It outlined the horizon. Its trees were tall, black figures like a city without lights, as if on the verge of inspiration, ready to be lit up. He walked towards it.

Marianne clung to the tree and fanned her small wings for a while. She had been right. It was unmistakable. There was something between Ansley and Beatrice, even if Ansley wasn't aware of it yet, Beatrice's admiration could easily become the hope that Ansley so desperately needed. And why shouldn't it? Why did this bother her? Hadn't she chosen Dex? She and Dex had been through so much together, and yet, throughout the years she often thought of Ansley and now, here he was, alive. He was alive and intense. Dex was many things, fun and adventurous, but he was not intense. Dedicated, yes, but not intense. He did not look at her as though he wanted to devour her. He did not write poetry. He did not risk his life to impress her. Oh stop it, she said to herself. So what? She flew up as high as possible so that the mist and cloud could blow away her fickle brain. There was more at stake here than silly idolatry. Dex loved her. She didn't need worship. Ansley was obsessive and he would suffocate her. Wouldn't he?

31

It's not easy raising an infant, especially in a swamp, and Jude fretted that the cherubs would harm Emoli out of jealousy, so he had him constantly under the spider's security. Fortunately the spiders adored him, as did the mutant fish, and he was learning how to swim beautifully. He wore his bubble like an oxygen mask and had learned to do little clicking dances with his legs to communicate to the spiders.

Jude's time spent with Emoli had changed him considerably, for it had meant that he had to watch, and endure, Emoli's development. Jude had never watched something grow before. He had always been impatient and eaten or taken what he wanted when he wanted it. It made him consider his own development and if it's true that like attracts like, it's certainly true that lost finds lost. Before he had franchised evil, he had definitely been lost. Lost to the garden and lost to his peer group, but also lost paternally, for he was the spawn of reactive minerals, and minerals are impassive. They never loved him. He did what he had to do to survive, but also, he did what he had to do to feel important. And he had felt important, powerful, but he had never been loved. Feared, yes, but not loved like the spiders loved Emoli.

It made him think. The truth is that he never wholly wanted to be a land dweller. Why else would he have spent so much time in that frigging tree?! It was expected of him, you see. It was expected that he should be a land dweller because he was a snake. In the end, most creatures do the thing expected of them, even vile renegades like himself, but if he had a dream it would be for wings, it would be for more than fear from eyes that looked into his, not love, mind you. Love would be pushing it, but something companionable, something similar to the gaze he received from Emoli. But then, he reminded himself, that kid does live in a bubble and you just never know how it will turn out with sheltered children. So, never mind, scratch that thought and move forward, but only three-quarters of him listened. But, he supposed it was to be expected, after all, it's downright difficult to maintain clout when you reach omnipotence. "Even my own self wants a piece of me!" he shouted to nobody, "It doesn't make any sense!"

32

They had been walking in the dark for hours. The air was full of fumes and Beatrice could hardly see in front of her own face. The moon was cloaked in cloud like a barely lit semicircle of a nearly evaporated drinks ring.

"How do you feel?" Beatrice asked Oren.

"A bit woozy actually, what about you?"

"Woozy too. The sand feels different as well. Sticky almost."

It was as if little balls of glue were periodically dropped across the ground. Beatrice stepped on another one and this time it stuck to her foot. She bent down to remove it from her shoe. She pressed it between her fingers and brought it up to her nose to smell.

"Tar," she said to Oren. "Here smell."

"That's tar alright." He began searching his pockets for his fire charm. When he found it he lift it up into the air. It shone like a blue star in his hand.

"Would you look at that," he said, as he waved his hand around slowly.

"What in the world is it?" Beatrice asked.

As far as the eye could see there were bubbling pools of tar like blistering burnt marks across the bottom of a frying pan, miles and miles of flat tar swamp. Beatrice bent down and held her hand over one.

"It's boiling hot Oren. What will we do? I really don't want to waste the charm here, but I can't think of another way to navigate this place. Can you? Oren? Oren where are you going? Wait! Wait for me!"

Oren was scrambling around the tar pools with his nose to the air like a hound following a scent. Then Beatrice saw them and knew instantly what they were. The objects of his fascination. A procession of fire-eaters twirled and deftly skipped around the tar pools like a herd of mad black gazelle. From their mouths spat puffs of fire, inside which small pixyish figures danced. Every once in a while the fire would form a hand that waved Oren onward. The fire-eaters themselves were like sinews of smoke. They twirled batons and hoops of infernos. Their drums commanded the flames. It increased with the beating increased and slowed with the beating slowed. Like black ghosts they danced inside the fire rings. Oren reached the One, who blew the fire hands to beckon him. He willingly gave him his fire charm. The One laughed a smoky laugh and threw it to a friend. Soon they were playing catch with the charm while Oren just stared at a woman whizzing through a fire ring. Beatrice tried not to look. She stumbled carefully on all fours around the tar pits trying to reach Oren. Suddenly the One saw her with his silver eyes, then laughed, breathed in a puff of smoke, and hissed fire at her like a dragon. She ducked away just in time but the tar pool next to her burst into flames. The One did it again, this time in quick succession, three more pools were blazing. There was nowhere for her to go. Fire was all around her. She could no longer see Oren. She screamed out his name but he was gone, seduced.

She knew she had to stand up and watch where they were going but all around her was fire. She could feel her skin begin to blister. I will not die, she said aloud. With all her might she forced herself to stand. The smoke burned her eyes and tears ran freely down her cheeks. She shouted for Oren again but it was useless. She could just make out a blue haze in the distance. She saw something large near it. What was it? It looked like an old water tower. Maybe there was water still in it? The obsidian arrow seared against her chest. It was in her breast pocket. Without thinking she grabbed it and threw it in the air towards the water tower. It did exactly as she willed it to do. Like a dart that grew and grew until it was the size of a small aircraft that broke and cracked open the water tower. Beatrice could hardly believe there was actually water left inside. It came pouring out and immediately extinguished the fire all around her. Suddenly the night was pitch black. The One became furious and sucked all of the wisps of fire-eaters into himself as if he were a large smoke sack. Beatrice could see Oren bobbing around inside. The sack thickened and thickened like a black sauce. Beatrice could only catch glimpses of Oren tumbling through it as the sack began to move and pull through the night. His face was rolling with the others. She couldn't see a thing and soon she couldn't see the sack. Help me, she whispered. In a flash her leopard was there and she clambered onto his back. Soundlessly and nimbly they followed the sack. Beatrice felt the last arrow against her chest and she knew what she had to do. They would just have to think of another way to pierce Jude. She had to save Oren. She waited until she caught sight of him dipping, then threw the arrow with all her might. It zapped the sack and they all came tumbling through the sky like black marbles. Many sizzled inside the streams of water, while others landed in the tar pools, lighting them once again. Oren was headed towards a blazing pool.

"There he is!" Beatrice shouted, and the leopard sprang underneath him, catching him moments before he landed in the fire.

He lay limp across the leopard. Beatrice had to hang on to him as they dodged fireballs and tar pools. The One was screaming mad and chasing them while hurling fireballs from his mouth. The leopard was fast, but the One was faster and soon caught up with them. Beatrice could feel his hot breath on her bare scalp every time he blew a fireball. Ahead she could see something shimmering and she prayed it was water. She clung to the leopard's neck, as well as to Oren who was beginning to slip. They had reached the edge of the tar pits, but the One was still heartily pursuing them and seemed to anticipate their every move. Yes, the shimmering definitely was water, and a few feet away from its surface, she shouted for the leopard to stop.

The leopard stopped abruptly. The One wasn't as quick and piloted into the water with a sizzle. He screeched a horrible gasping, raspy screech and diluted like a drop of ink in a water glass. His eyes were the only things that remained, like two silver stones that slowly began to sink. The leopard and Beatrice watched them sink all the way to the bottom. They were breathless. The leopard nodded and vanished.

Oren woke up.

"What happened?" he asked, rubbing his head.

"You idiot!" Beatrice slapped Oren across the cheek. "Seduced by fire-eaters? For goodness sake Oren, we lost our arrows! How will we pierce Jude now?!"

"I am so sorry. I don't know what came over me. It was like I was possessed."

"You were possessed! I almost died out there you know. You would have just let me burn to death. Some hero you are."

"That's a bit harsh. I was out of control, I told you, I couldn't help myself."

"Be quiet! Honestly I don't want to hear your pathetic excuses. I don't want to hear you period."

"But Beatrice … "

"Shut it."

"Fine I won't … "

"Zip."

They walked in silence. The green smoke seemed inconceivably distant. It coiled between horizon and cloud like a single northern light, a radiant portal only they could see. They walked, side by side, but not touching. Their eyes gently bouncing like four suns on the same orbit. They didn't take their eyes off the smoke. They didn't speak for over an hour. Their feet pressed against the flat land and their moon shadows were long and uninterrupted. It seemed unnecessary to speak, as if the sound waves their voices would introduce might disrupt the straight flat line that connected them to the smoke. Houses lay broken in pieces and tilted as if they'd been dropped from the sky and crashed. Wrecks were everywhere. A wreck of a village. A wreck of a stable. All the animals were gone. Beatrice pictured them hiding in clusters behind the wrecks like schools of fish. She saw them as colorful, tropical almost, rainbows with eyes against the gray sky.

***

Once, in the early days, she and her protector had stayed in a small house next to a pond. Swimming in the pond was fearfully exhilarating. She never knew if it had been a fish or a reed that had brushed up against her legs and she loved the pond for its penetrable mystery. A middle-aged woman lived in the house and had invited them to stay. She had found them camping in the woodland. Early morning, from the safety of her sleeping bag, Beatrice had heard a soft crunching underfoot, a sucking in of breath then footsteps backing up and scattering away. She knew the sounds of deer. Beatrice knew it was a human and suspected it was a woman on account of its gentleness. Later that afternoon the woman approached them with sandwiches. The bread was warm and the meat fresh. She must have decided that danger didn't travel with a small girl and invited them in for a hot drink. She taught Beatrice to swim along the reeds like an otter. She said there were many kinds of carp in that pond. She asked no questions. Perhaps the war was reason enough for everything.

"A mystery is more romantic than the truth," she said.

"Take this, for example, I found this book by the pond."

She held up the spine of an enormous volume of twentieth-century paintings.

"One day it wasn't there and the next it was. No sign of human occupancy that I could see, just this book on modern painting. And look around you," she said, as she waved her arms to indicate the walls covered with torn-out pages of landscape paintings.

"It is my salvation. When it all fades," she pointed out the window. "When it all fades, I will still have it here. If you can see something you can keep it real. Yet where did the book come from? I've thought of many possibilities but most probably it was dropped by mistake from someone running from something to somewhere. I don't want to know exactly. The point is you never know what will be the thing that saves you or when you'll find it," she said, and gazed out the window.

The light on her cheekbone flickered in the fire. It was her own reflection she saw in the night.

"There were once so many trout in that pond you wouldn't believe it," she said, to break the silence. "I wasn't lonely then."

Out of the dawn, rocks seem to stumble towards them. Of course, they are unmoving, but perception is everything, her protector used to say. He said it when they left the woman with her pond of reeds. He said she was lonely enough to give them up. That lonely people will do reckless things to stir themselves. They snuck out one night. Quiet as swallows. Beatrice wondered if she thought of them as mysteries too. Once they were there and then they were gone.

"Are we speaking yet? I'm getting hungry and would like some of that apple cake Dex packed for us," Oren said.

"Alright. Just don't leave me to die again," Beatrice said.

"I'll try. As long as you don't get too annoying," Oren said, and winked.

They sat down on a large rock and unwrapped the cake.

"Oh my God this is delicious," Beatrice said.

Oren went to open his mouth to speak and crumbs fell out.

"Slow down little piggy," Beatrice laughed.

"Possession makes you hungry," Oren said.

Beatrice opened her bag and took out Ansley's book of poems.

"Is that the book from your boyfriend?" Oren said.

"He's not my boyfriend Oren. You are such a child."

"My mistake, sorry," he said sarcastically.

"We just like the same things. It's like a mutual appreciation. I wouldn't expect you to understand an intellectual connection."

"I know all about connections, believe me. The thing is, you are a Grower Bea. In three days' time you'll be blown to smithereens and he'll be god knows what, but the likelihood of you two seeing one another again is basically nil."

"I know, I know what you say is true, but."

"But what?"

"Well it feels nice to be close to a human."

"What do you mean? We're human-ish."

"No we're not Oren, we're vessels, pawns, holding cells, we run and hide. We are too miraculous to be human, too precious, like breakable vases, we simply survive to carry. I can't tell you how often I have longed for fervor or creativity."

"Really? Well I for one am happy to leave the humans behind, damnable species to be honest, mucked up everything."

"They weren't so bad. It's just that so much depends on who you listen to. If humans could be forgiven for one thing it would be their ingenuity."

"I suppose Ansley was ingenious?"

"Art is the greatest form of ingenuity and yes, he was, how else could he have lived while surviving? It's honourable to live creatively when the rest of the world is merely trying to survive. It's what I longed for, what was missing, I mean, just listen to this:

Evolution
Inside sunlight shuttles down the long corridor
of memory, dead, yet waiting to feed
like meat hanging in a window, that hook
still in us, still searching,

only changing the beast, only lonely,
even so, moments.
Moments exist where we skin
our old selves, where we touch,
and make leaps.

"Isn't that remarkable?"

"Yeah it is. Look. I get what you're saying, I do, it's just that I never needed anything like that. I don't know, I liked the running, the constant challenge, the life on the edge. It really thrilled me. But we are different. And, as the saying goes, it takes all kinds. Just as long as you know it will never last."

"Does anything?"

He looked out over the hills of rock stained with burnt patches. The sky was so heavy that it sat on the horizon in one big gritty block. Occasionally a scrap of tall grass would emerge uncomfortably from the ground like a monster's head.

"Remember the trees?"

"Yeah," said Oren. "You're right. Nothing stays the same."

33

Stepping into the forest was like stepping into a hot skin suit. The air was membrane thick and waterlogged his lungs, which he imagined as two pink sponges he would ring out as soon as he'd collected these blasted seeds. He looked up. The trees were fathomless towers that vines coiled around as thick as thighs. It was true that you could actually watch the vines grow and hear them crunch as they gripped the bark. The sound reminded Ansley of a cat chewing a rabbit's skull. It felt malicious and intentional how the vines squeezed out the light and he sensed that without light he might die, an extraordinary idea for a man who had lived his life in darkness. His pale, squinty eyes searched the canopy and found, to his great relief, a lime-colored winnow of sunlight. Delicious, as if the sun were a fruit that had been squeezed and this particular trickle of sunlight were a stream of juice sliding down a green forearm just for him. He opened his mouth to taste it. It was diluted enough that it could touch him painlessly. He stood inside the weak sunlight with the forest pressed against his throat like a hand, and yet, despite the circumstances, he recalled each glorious time he'd had the sun on his face and so felt instantly renewed.

Help me, he mouthed, because he felt that luck might be listening. And he needed no shortage of help. These forests can smell a mammal a mile away. He tried not to think about what the forest did to mammals. He concentrated on the light.

Light, a soft hand cupping his face, he thought to himself, day as metaphor. If the sun burns your skin you learn to carry it in your pocket. His body is a white sack he stuffs ideas into, for instance, the idea of mid-afternoon glittering across the water or white thunderheads in a blue sky. The possibilities a pink dawn can bring. These ideas shelve themselves inside his ribcage like unread books. They insulate him. He has made a study out of insulating himself, which is why he had agreed to help the Growers, for it's one thing to keep from feeling and another to remain useless to the world. He had always felt that greatness, true usefulness, was hibernating inside him like a wrathful white bear. Now was his chance.

***

When the war began he was a young boy that lived on the edge of a deep green wood, a short distance from the sea. Often he heard seagulls scraping their cries like fingernails down a distant sky. The soil had chalk in it that caused white flotsam to swirl across the streams as globs of thickened clouds. Elf meringue, he had named it, though there was no one to share this with. He was squatting by the stream, gently bouncing his finger against a large piece of meringue caught on a stick, when he heard the first missiles. It was rare to hear anything mechanical, now that the oil was gone, and at first he thought they were the seagulls. Then the ground shook like an animal waking beneath it. Ausley fell back and the meringue broke free. He watched it float downstream for a long time before he rose and walked back to the house. On the hill beyond the village, he saw a sizzling hole the size of a ship. When he opened his door his father held him tight.

His father had hunted deer. They'd hung dripping in the garage before they were chopped into venison. He would enter the garage, navigate carefully around the pools of blood, and close their eyes. Their lashes were long and tickly soft as spider legs. Their velvet faces were like elves. It was the first he knew of beauty and theirs was a world he wanted to enter.

Once he came across a deer's bed in the bracken. He sat inside it, fingered the fallen bits of hair, which were coarser then he had expected. The bracken fronds had an oily residue that made them soft. The smell was warm and feral, the smell intoxicated Ansley and he lay down, curled like a fetus, listening to the twitch of the insects, and fell asleep. When he woke she was there standing beside him and looking off into the distance. A pure white doe. He rose to a seated position and she turned her head slowly to look at him, intense as a spell. She did not flinch. Her eyes were rabbit pink, like his only graceful and knowing. He envied her confidence. She was the one his father had called the devil. She spooked him just as Ansley spooked him, so he wouldn't shoot her for fear of ill luck, but Ansley had seen her eyes were full of gentleness. The following spring she gave birth to an albino fawn, white as the driven snow, and they lived longer than all the others, perhaps their offspring are living still, for war can burn many traits out of a man but superstition is not one of them. Ansley understood this. He has learnt that sometimes if you carry a burden differently it becomes a float. The nights were cold in London and the streets Ansley walked down were filled with men sitting in circles around fires. Their red-golden faces whispered from shadowed, seemingly disconnected bodies. They wouldn't look at him. Instead they waited until he had walked past then shot long stares at him like hot pokers, his body a colander their fear drained though. The beauty of being a freak is invincibility. Nobody dared to touch him. Many meals were given to him on account of his curse, of course they were given out of fear, but he ate them nevertheless.

It had always been this way.

And now this. What could he even call it? This closing forever of the old ideas. Like when the streetlamps finally stopped working and the city revealed a new city inside its own light. He was the same, this place was the same, it was all the same, except that he saw differently. Perception is in the layering, he wrote inside his makeshift notebook, and put it back into his pocket. It lay next to Beatrice's hair. Beatrice. Beatrice was extraordinary and normal at the same time, she was touchable, reachable, and illuminating sunshine. But he had always loved Marianne.

And the layers now shriveled like old skins on the floor. There was an opportunity now. A mere chance that he and Marianne might return as something else, some other form, how he longed to take another form. One that she could love, not just admire, but a sinking into the skull, a pistol against the throat love that renders one helpless.

34

Ansley penetrated deeper and deeper into the phosforest. The air was dense and the sound it made as it rubbed against his skin and in and out of his lungs was that of grating sandpaper. After a few steps he had to sit down and rest. It was as if he couldn't get enough oxygen into his lungs. Giant heliflies, like horseflies the size of model helicopters, patrolled the phosforest searching for mammals but fortunately he could hear them before he could see them. One was heading straight towards him. He looked around for a place to hide and crouched down behind an enormous fern. He accidently stepped on a toadstool lying beneath the undergrowth. Tiny red insects puffed up like a blast of gas and covered his face. He tried to brush them off, but they were like soot, so the more he brushed, the more they smeared, and soon the red stains began to burn. He wiped harder but it only rubbed the burn in, like chilies, they seared his eyes and skin. He wanted to scream, to run to the stream he'd seen a few yards back, but he was trapped. The helifly had stopped, its eyes suspiciously orbited the area with clicking lenses. Its long tongue extended towards the fern causing the ferns fronds to sizzle. It came whisper close to Ansley. He could see only out of his left eye as his right was completely swollen and seeping acidic liquid. He had to bite his tongue to keep from crying, from breathing. Blood pooled in his mouth and ran down his chin. Don't drip, don't make a noise, don't drip. He tried to close his mouth but his tongue was too swollen. What was that? He had seen something move and shake the ferns. He could have sworn he had seen a face. He worried that soon he might not be able to breathe. He felt his left eye closing as the helifly licked the air around him, searching for the best place to pierce. Ansley held the needle in his hand. It was as swollen as a funfair balloon. The helifly reared back, preparing to strike. It looked as though it was going for the neck. Ansley lifted his arm with enormous effort and stuck the needle into his neck moments before the helifly's tongue stabbed. Immediately his neck ballooned and the helifly slurped the blood. Satisfied, it rolled its tongue in like a garden hose, snap, and flew away. Ansley laughed a wheezing laugh, he couldn't believe the needle had worked, and passed out.

***

He woke in unbearable pain. His right eye was completely swollen shut and his left eye swollen to a small slit through which Ansley could just see a miasma of shaded gray movements. He heard a commotion, a rustling, like many feet. He tried to turn his head but it was too painful. He tried to speak but felt something hard in his mouth. He pursed his lips around it like sucking a straw and breathed. He became aware of his throat. It seemed to grip around this straw, which made it impossible to speak, but he dared not take it out for fear he'd be unable to breathe.

In his warehouse, he often woke with the feeling that someone was in the room, but when he looked he found only the same emptiness. "Who are you," he'd shout at the emptiness, of course there was no answer, save a shaping darkness, a crouched loss. The dark, he wanted to say, keep me in the dark, but again lost consciousness.

35

The buried house showed only its shingles and stood protected as an armadillo in the morning's white sun. It felt remarkably derelict. The green smoke poured from behind it like a leaking stab wound. Beatrice began to dig. She uncovered the top of the door.

"Look at this," she said to Oren, as she rubbed her hand down the recent hatchet marks. "Look at these marks, what do you think they mean?"

"Somebody has been here," he said, and started digging as well.

A long, low growl came from inside the house. It sounded menacing and Beatrice stopped.

"What the heck is that?"

"Probably just strays," Oren said.

"Dogs? Do you think they'll attack us?'

"I'm not sure but we need to get her out of there all the same."

"I feel really uneasy about this Oren."

"So do I but what else can we do?"

"Something is definitely wrong."

"Tell me about it," he said.

"Do you think she's …" she didn't want to use the word "dead."

"I hope not," he said, and started digging again. The growl increased and Beatrice could hear the jaws snap at the wall behind where Oren dug. Beatrice walked around the back of the house to see if there was an easier access. It was strange how the smoke was seeping, as if it wasn't coming directly from the house but rolling past it and up into the air. Again she thought of a leaking wound.

"Wait Oren," she called, "I think the smoke has been detoured somehow. Let's just try shouting for Valentine, maybe she isn't in the house after all, you know? There is a haze of smoke here, have a look."

Oren came over. He was covered in sweaty sand and shook himself like a dog.

"Stop it! That's disgusting," she said.

He smiled then shouted, "Valentine?"

Beatrice called for her as well. "Valentine? Are you here?"

"Listen," said Beatrice. There was a tapping, faint but regular. "Where is that coming from?" she said, with her ear to the ground. "Here! Dig!"

They uncovered a small opening as if a pipe had been stuck in the ground ten feet from the house. Smoke billowed from it along with the stench of something awful.

"Bullseye," said Oren. "Now fingers crossed she's there."

""Valentine?" Beatrice shouted down the pipe.

"Is that really you?" Came a small voice from below.

"Oh, Valentine we've found you! Are you alright?" Beatrice was shocked that the voice was that of a child. She hadn't expected a child.

"How do I know it's you?" Valentine asked.

"I'm Beatrice, a Grower like yourself and Oren is here as well."

"Is that all?"

"Of course."

"How can I be sure?"

"Let's see. I know your protector gave you a telescope."

"Anybody could know that," Valentine said.

"Ok. I know you cried seeds after your protector died."

"We were never told we'd cry seeds," her voice broke in a sob.

"I know, I know, it was a shock."

"So many shocks," again her voice trailed off in a sob.

"Valentine I'm coming down. I think I can just about fit. Oren will stay up here and be on the lookout okay?"

She dangled her feet inside and began to jump.

"Wait, what if you can't get back out? What will I do?" Oren asked.

"I'm sure you think of something. Besides, we can't just leave her down there and your pancake belly won't fit through this hole."

"Just be careful. I'll wait here."

Beatrice saluted and jumped down into a huge drum-like metal cavern. Valentine sat sobbing in the corner and when Beatrice approached the low growl began again. She saw it was a fox. A fox with barred teeth.

"It's alright," Valentine told the fox, and he knelt beside her.

"Is he your pet?" Beatrice asked.

"Nobody owns foxes," she said, disgusted.

"Of course, I'm sorry, is he your friend then?"

"My very, very best friend."

"That's lovely Valentine, listen, we need to get out of here, will you be able to manage it? Are you hurt?"

"I'm not leaving without Fox," she said, and wiped her nose on her sleeve. "What about her?" she asked, and pointed in the direction of her protector.

"First I need to know if you're hurt Valentine," and she tried approaching her again but the fox stopped her.

"No, I'm just scared."

"What happened?"

"A machine came and it started clawing at us and then she, she died," she started sobbing again.

"I'm so sorry Valentine, but we're here now and we will keep you safe. Your protector is waiting for us too you know," she pulled the pouch from her pocket. It was papery to the touch and when she opened it, it dissolved her hands. A large bumble bee flew out and over to the resting body. It sat on the forehead. Suddenly an enormous swarm curled in from the pipe's opening and completely covered the body. Valentine looked up and sobbed even more. The fox made a funny noise deep in his throat. The protector's body hummed and then disappeared. There was silence but for a distant grinding. It's that noise again thought Beatrice. Valentine completely stopped crying and looked up at Beatrice in horror.

"That's it, that's the machine, it's come back!" she shrieked and scrambled back into the corner

"Hey there's something funny up here," Oren shouted down the hole.

"Quick Oren squeeze down here!" said Beatrice.

"Are you kidding?"

"Then hide Oren, hide!"

The fox darted down a long tunnel.

"Where is he going?"

"To get your friend," said Valentine.

"Oren follow the fox!" shouted Beatrice, then two minutes later, "Can you hear me? Oren? Oren?"

"I'm here," said Oren, panting behind her. The fox was there too.

"That was quick. Where did he lead you?"

"Through a series of tunnels," he began to explain but was cut off by the noise. "Have you been digging a burrow?" he asked Valentine.

She nodded, "A burrow hive," she said, "shhh, there it is again," she was terrified.

Beatrice went to her and this time the fox let her pass. She held her. Oren sat opposite them in complete silence. The grinding came closer and closer like something out of a nightmare. The ground shook and you could hear the claws gnash and cut into the earth like teeth. The machine was close now and the grinding pitch high enough to be piercing, deafening. Little spittles of sand sprayed down the hole every time the machine moved. It made Valentine shake. It was definitely looking for something, someone. Beatrice held the girl even closer. Her arms were so small and thin. She was only eight at the most. She had lived through nothing but war. Valentine hid her face in the nape of Beatrice's neck. Beatrice stroked her hair, the grease on it was so thick it had turned waxy at the scalp. A film of it covered Beatrice's neck and clavicles like a lotion. There was something so unloved about Valentine that it made Beatrice ache. Beatrice could see the blades of the claw lower and scrape over the covering of the hole. Valentine screamed but the noise was lost in the grind. A large helifly entered the hole and circumnavigated the drum. They each slunk into the shadows and froze. Valentine could not help whimpering as the helifly began its inspection with its strange prism eyes. The swarm of bees silently returned and coated each of the Growers' bodies like a shield. Their breathing quickened but they didn't move a single muscle. The helifly stopped in front of Oren and pierced its tongue into a bee near Oren's mouth. It sucked and rolled its tongue back in again. It seemed satisfied, but confused. Suddenly it spun around and pierced the fox. The bees hadn't covered the fox and the helifly tasted the blood of a mammal. It lashed its tongue out again like an iguana's, rolled the fox back to its mouth and zapped up and out of the pipe.

"No!" screamed Valentine, rushing to the hole. She held her arms up in the shaft of sunlight as if it would beam her up. "The ladder! Where's the ladder?!"

She searched frantically along the walls of the drum, her hands moved ahead of her with vigor as if she'd been momentarily blinded by the sunlight. Suddenly she produced a ladder and began to position it when Oren stopped her.

"We will all die if you chase after him," he said, "I'm sorry but I can't let you do that."

Valentine collapsed like a puppet thrown onto the floor. Oren looked at Beatrice and nodded towards Valentine, when miraculously the fox whimpered at the pipes opening.

"That's him! We must get him!" Valentine jumped up and down.

"Wait until the machine leaves and I'll get him for you," Beatrice told her. Already the machine's grind was distancing, and when they couldn't hear it anymore, Beatrice placed the ladder up the hole and climbed to the top.

"Wait here," she said, before she disappeared.

Seconds later she returned with the fox in her arms and climbed down the ladder. He was bruised and weak, but very much alive.

"I think he'll be fine," she said, as she placed him in Valentine's arms. "He is one tough cookie," then she turned to Oren, "I can only guess that they didn't want him."

"No, they were looking for me," Valentine said, as she stroked the fox's fur.

"They were looking for all of us," Oren put a hand on Valentine's shoulder.

"It is diabolical up there. As if a giant mouth had come and chomped through everything," Beatrice told Oren.

"Then it's best that we stay down here for a while, at least until sunset. Valentine can use my shirt as a sling to carry the fox and we'll head towards the final smoke signal. Besides she needs her tattoo anyway," Oren said.

"Do you think the moths will come and get us?"

"Not this time, I'm not sure they'd find us and anyway it's too dangerous with that thing out there. What is this place anyway?" he asked Valentine, as he looked around.

"An old rainwater harvester," she told him, and he laughed.

"What's so funny?"

"It's just that I've been sitting in fox poo for the last half an hour in a bathtub with no water, seems ironic doesn't it?"

Beatrice and Valentine laughed. It felt good to be laughing. Beatrice pulled a few bananas out of her stomach and handed one to the astonished Valentine.

"Good thinking, let's eat," said Oren.

"How did you do that?" asked Valentine.

"You just wait," said Beatrice. "You just wait."

36

Ansley woke inside a deep, room-sized chamber covered with vines, as if he'd been hidden. The phosforest was a snake pit of vines and roots. It bounced when you walked on it as if you were walking on shredded tires and rubber rings. He could see clearly out of one eye but the other one was still swollen shut. He looked up through a small bowl-shaped hole to the sky. It was pale green, a murky mint pool where dark green leaves, long and large as sharks, swam back and forth in the breeze. With great pain he looked around himself.

He lay in a circle of bizarre objects: thimbles, rusted nails, various rodent teeth, shiny gum wrappers, an old socket, blue telephone wires, and a child's toy car. Alarm bells went off in Ansley's head. Where was he? He still couldn't move his body.

"Hello?" he called, but couldn't see a single person.

"Hello," a voice answered.

Ansley tried to lift his head and promptly collapsed with pain. A figure moved out of the corner and towards him.

"You're human," Ansley said. "But how?"

"Never mind," the voice said. "You're weak, take this."

A small bird jumped down from the shadow's shoulder and landed beside Ansley's face. It had a large seed in its mouth that it thrust down Ansley's throat. Ansley choked but swallowed the seed anyhow.

"What the hell!" he shouted, then instantly began to feel woozy. His body relaxed into the pain that dissipated like a puddle dissolving into the soil. He saw double and was too exhausted to fight or hide.

"That's right, sleep," the voice said.

The bird hopped around his head. It was as if it were organizing something. But Ansley was dizzy, so many birds hopped around his head. He hadn't heard or seen a single bird since he entered the phosforest. What was it doing here? As if to answer the bird hopped right up to his good eye, opened its mouth, and out came the screech of a police siren, followed by the sound of a doorbell then a human laugh. Ansley recognized the laugh as his own.

"I know you." His speech was slurred. "You're one of those mimic birds, what are they called? A lyrebird. Is that right? I can't believe this."

The lyrebird made the sound of a car alarm and displayed his frayed tail plumage. Ansley saw that most of the feathers had been burnt off.

"Looks like we've both had a rough time of it," said Ansley, and the seed finally kicked in and Ansley passed out.

Outside a swarm of heliflies soldiered through the air and the low grind of a distant machine came closer, closer.

He dreamt of Beatrice.

She had painted a bird on the ceiling above his pillow. She had painted the whole room, each wall a different season. Moths were holding up a hundred tiny painting of flowers. They hovered as though they were swaying in the wind. She had painted grassy fields. A bluebell, the stem curving its neck with the weight of the little blue lanterns. Next are white snowdrops clustered underneath an oak tree. The English oak looks as though a child had drawn it, round and bulbous at the top, almost like a billowing bud-filled cloud with a straight strong trunk. She had painted a pale-blue spider's web in the grass. Daffodils. A nest of eggs. Turquoise spring. On the next wall she had painted summer. The oak cloud is lush and green. The raspberries are ripe for picking. There are yellow roses and oxeye daisies. He could almost smell the honeysuckle wrapping around the trunk. The sky is a deep blue. On the autumn wall the sky is as orange as a pumpkin. The leaves are bright red like the sun. Vines of squash and piles of leaves. Rudbeckia blazes in full flower. The winter branches cut up a white sky. Underneath the snowy ground green waits patiently beside a sleeping fox. The birds and deer like sharp outlines in the sky. Black shadows in white air like crystal clear ideas. Things are hidden, and equally, things are unable to hide. On his bedpost hung her crystal necklace, to catch the sun she had painted.

When he woke and saw his room he could have cried.

It was like waking inside a garden. He had done that once. He had jumped the fence of a private garden and slept beneath the canopy of a bright yellow azalea. He had just arrived in London. He had thought the house was abandoned because the front windows had been boarded up, however, when he woke he saw a man, frail, yet unmoving, staring at him from the garden window. The man opened the garden door without taking his eyes off Ansley and suddenly an enormous dog dashed across the garden with his spitty teeth bared. Ansley jumped the fence just in time.

In Beatrice's garden he took his time waking up. He savored it.

"Annsleee," she drew his name out. His mother must have spoken his name like this once, more a cloud than a sound escaping her lips, wispy and light. It hovered in the air and vanished. Even the mouth can forget. It was as if she reminded him of things he never knew to know, like how the sun lures steam from the rock, there were cracks in his hard self through which, vaporously, words rose then disappeared. But he saw them. He felt their hot breath. And it made him want to scrape the dead, old and sharp as barnacles, out. And it made him make promises like secrets written backwards. They were hers to discover, to decode. "Annsleee," like pulling on a clean shirt.

"Have you ever seen sunlight?" she had asked him.

Only the dappled light of woodland in the height of summer and once in an abandoned barn. He'd slept on the damp hay and in the morning light streamed through the cobwebs and he held out his hand

and touched it. And sometimes on the back of a fish. When he was a child, he'd sit at the edge of the pond and wait for the fish to flick up from the dark roots to the surface. Their scales were sewn together with a light that seemed inviolable, deep, for there is something archaic about a fish. They know what they know. And sometimes moments rise, like bubbles, like memories, where you think they'll tell you but instead they offer the chase. The chase is more than the answer, the fish seem to grin, yet for him they carried the sun on their backs and made it alive.

He knew what he knew.

And most of it was wrapped in shadow, most of it was black, but for the rare fish flicking to the surface and surprising him with its radiance, which reflected his radiance, his light, and just as if his eyes were portholes, he watched this light glistening inside him. A promise for a better future, a promise for importance drawn from, learned from his suffering. He felt he could tell her this. He felt that Beatrice might understand. How a stir can thread a halted heart like a river threads the land, connecting places and engraving.

37

Ansley thought he could hear hoof beats but it was only the blood pounding in his head. He could see out of both eyes now and could lift his body with little pain. He could sit up easily enough but the vines above him like a roof of joined arms made it impossible to stand without banging his head. The same strange collection of objects encircled him. He picked up the toy car and studied it curiously. He noticed movement in a far corner and, quite suddenly, a small figure appeared before him. A child, slender and silver white. In its hair it wore a large yellow paperclip. It reminded Ansley of himself except the child had dark-brown eyes and long white hair. On its shoulder it carried the lyrebird. A phosforest pirate, thought Ansley, whatever next?

"Hello," Ansley said.

"Hello," the child answered, while replicas of this child began appearing from the shadowed vines to encircle him. A world of them it seemed. Each as translucent as a pale inner wrist. The only difference was that the leader wore the yellow paperclip.

"What's your name?" Ansley asked the leader.

"Carson, and yours?"

"Ansley. Thank you for healing me Carson," he said, as he stuck out his hand.

"You're welcome," Carson said.

"What was that pill you gave me?" Ansley asked.

"A pig weed pill and pig weed sap for your skin. It's very greedy and eats anything in its path."

"I see. Glad I didn't know when I was eating it, not that Mr. Mimic gave me the chance to refuse, but, well, thanks again."

"Why are you here?" Carson stomped his foot like an angry child.

"Now wait a minute. You don't have to shout or get upset. I'm not here to harm anyone. I am here for a fruit, actually the seeds inside a certain fruit, it's called the plasmid tree – do you know it? Can you help me?"

Carson said nothing.

"You must know it. It's the biggest tree in the forest I'm told. Perhaps it is the source of other medicines? Can I speak to your parents?"

"You think we're children?"

"Well, yes, aren't you?"

"We are not children. We have not been children for many years, but are stuck in adolescence so we don't reproduce. You said this tree was one of medicine, so will this fruit allow us to mature?"

"I don't know to be honest. Maybe. It works like a transmitter of genes so it's possible. Then you must know the tree?"

"We know the tree but it's protected by a god."

"Like a god you can see?"

"Yes. It is very dangerous."

"Does that mean you won't help me?"

"We have come close to this tree before."

"You only have to show me where it is. I will handle the god and the fruit picking. Can you do that?"

"It is still dangerous. The god might see us."

"What if I gave you this? " Ansley remembered the red barrette he'd collected the night Beatrice and Oren had found him. He took it from his pocket and handed it to Carson. His eyes lit up at the sight of the hairclip. Quickly he snatched it from Ansley's hand and inspected it. Greed, Ansley thought, is innate.

"We will help you," he whispered, still stroking the hairclip.

The sooner the better, he thought to himself, and stretched his legs. The others, mere wisps of white, gasped at Carson's words and quickly ran away.

From his pocket Ansley took the remainder of his notebook and a pencil.

Love
The idea peeked out
like a worm
from an eye socket.
It seemed the last,
the polish, underneath which
everything shone.

He wrote. Not knowing if he was writing to Marianne or Beatrice.

38

Marianne couldn't stay on the tree. The tree had a consciousness, so as soon as it discovered her outside of its interior, it would fold her back into the realm, where she would be watched. The moths were gathering as she'd told them to do, they flocked over each leaf and fanned their wings, testing the air, in preparation for the journey ahead. It was a long way to the phosforest and they had to be careful. Although she could shift, moths were delicate, and their protection was in numbers. As a whole, they rose into the air. Now was her chance to join them, she lifted off the branch and into a cloud of moths. The sound was unbelievable, wing brushing wing, the air and her brain were full of friction, she was so taken by the sound that she didn't see the fire sprites dancing below them. The One, known as Pele Agnimitra, threw up her flaming hoop, like a shooting star with a blazing tail that crystallized, netting the moths inside it. The hoop returned to Pele Agnimitra. From the palms of her hands she released tiny birds of fire that danced and entranced the moths into submission. Pele Agnimitra reached her hand into the net and searched, as if reading each moth, without burning a single moth wing, until she found Marianne. Then, she cusped the tiny blue pygmy moth gently and solidified into a woman with bright red hair and a tattered crimson dress, from the pocket of which she pulled a black candle. She lit the candle by blowing across its wick and placed Marianne inside the flame. She carried the candle as she walked towards the sea, with all of the sprites, still willows of smoke and dreamlike, blowing fire and dancing around her. The candle's flame was not hot, nor hurtful, but it was all consuming and exhausted Marianne into a deep, deep slumber. Behind her, the net dissipated into smoke and the moths fell into a giant, motionless pile. "They will wake," Pele whispered to the flame, "don't worry, sleep."

39

The machine had gone but the helifly was waiting, silent as a poacher, for its prey. Oren was the first to emerge from the harvester, and as soon as his head poked out, the helifly flicked his tongue and covered it like a sticky pink hood. Oren was yanked through the hole and pulled straight up into the air. He hadn't even the chance to scream but Beatrice did.

"Hey!" she shouted, and scurried up the ladder, "Oren!"

She took off running but it was futile. Her heart sank to see Oren hanging limp as a caught mouse from the tongue of the helifly as it clicked and whirled through the air. Oren was a hundred times its size, but the tongue was a net that the helifly carried with ease. She was out of breath. She ran until she collapsed. Oren and the helifly were growing smaller and smaller in the sky. She looked up and saw a tiny speck approaching, then heard a terrible shriek.

"The eagle! Look!" she pointed towards the eagle in the sky. Valentine and the fox came running up behind her, panting.

"Will it save him?" Valentine asked.

"It must, come on!" she said, and they ran towards Oren and the eagle.

A battle was taking place. The eagle swooped down with extended claws like blades and gashed at the helifly's tongue. But the helifly had a defence of its own. Its tongue split into two and it used its stinger like a needled snake striking at the eagle in the air. It was aiming for its heart. All the while Oren was dangling, rope-like legs whipped about in the air. Beatrice was afraid he'd already been killed. The stinger and the eagle crashed again and again in the sky. Each time the eagle's shriek flew down their ears like rockets. Valentine crouched on the ground holding her ears with her head down. The fox was under her. Beatrice grabbed a rock and threw it at the helifly. She missed. She grabbed another and threw again. This time she hit its needled tongue just before it stabbed the eagle. The helifly was alarmed, shocked he looked around at his other opponents. It was just the distraction the eagle needed. The eagle was able to wrap his claws around the helifly's tongue and tear it apart like a piece of liquorice. Oren dropped to the ground. Beatrice and Valentine ran to him. His head was still encased inside the helifly's tongue like a spitty pink balloon. Beatrice could see that he was alive inside of his air bubble.

"How do we get him out?" asked Valentine.

"I don't know," said Beatrice, as she tried to rip the balloon. Then the eagle flew down with the needle it had severed from the helifly and dropped it in front of Beatrice.

"Do I use this?"

The eagle just looked at her and hopped next to Oren's head. Beatrice took the needle and tried to gently pop the balloon but it was as thick as leather. She jabbed it and sliced a little of Oren's cheek.

"Oh no!" she cried, but the balloon was shriveling and soon his head was out in the open air. A trickle of blood ran down his cheek. He woke and put his hand to his face.

"What happened?" he asked. He was still a bit drowsy.

"I'm so sorry, I accidently cut your cheek when I was freeing you. I was just in such a hurry and so afraid, I'm sorry Oren," she was welling up with tears.

"Don't worry. You freed me didn't you?" He noticed the eagle. "Thank you, you saved me. Thank you."

The eagle pushed off the ground and flew away. They watched it grow as small as a pupil in the sun's eye.

Valentine and the fox went to where the helifly had fallen. It had burst into flames and fallen through the sky like a miniature airplane crash. Where it fell was burnt out and smouldering. Nothing was left of the helifly save a chip from its prism eye. Valentine picked it up and tied it to a piece of string she had around her neck. The chip was no bigger than a thumbnail. On the string she had tied many things. A mussel shell with a hole in it. A plastic red heart. A whistle.

Beatrice saw her.

"I collect feathers," she told Valentine, as she removed her towel from her backpack. "See?" .

She unrolled the towel revealing various feathers of all shapes and sizes. Valentine ran her fingers along the spines of two seagull feathers.

"I like this one the best," she said, about a small iridescent blue one.

"That's a kingfisher. It's the rarest one I've got," Beatrice answered.

"The eagle dropped a feather by the burnt helifly," Valentine said.

Beatrice rushed over to the site. Sure enough a large brown and white eagle feather lay perfectly preserved and flawless on the ground.

"It's beautiful," Beatrice said, as she caressed it. She carefully placed it in the towel, gently rolled it up, and put it away.

"Why don't you wear it? On you coat or something?" Valentine asked.

"When I had hair I used to tie it into a knot and sometime stick a feather in it. But I like being bald. Also I'm afraid to lose my feathers. Strange but they're the most precious things I've got." Plus Ansley's book, she thought to herself, but didn't tell Valentine.

"My necklace is precious to me."

"Yes, this war has made collectors of us all. As if we were collecting the ingredients for some magic potion to get us out of here. Or maybe we are the magic potions and we are just trying to make ourselves feel normal."

They walked back to Oren. The fox lay beside him.

"Looks like I've made a friend," Oren said, as they approached. "What did you find?"

"An eagle feather and a prism piece from the helifly's eye. How do you feel? Should we go back to the harvester and rest? I'm a bit worried about how exposed we are here. That helifly was told to stay by someone."

"Yeah I know. But that's why I don't want to go back to the harvester. What if someone or something comes looking for the helifly? They'll know just were to go and then we're sitting ducks."

"But will you be able to travel?" said Beatrice.

"Honestly, it's fine, I can walk. We are safer on the move anyway. The sun is getting lower and soon we'll see the smoke."

40

The new moon produced a night as black as any thought. The pale people reminded Ansley of silverfish the way they scurried and jammed against one another inside their coiled shadows. Their eyes twinkling out at him like frantic cats. There was a strange sense of boiling whenever they were huddled together, like silver bubbles in a black pot. They couldn't decide if he was a demon or a god and, it appeared, they thought staring at him would answer their questions. Ansley found it uncomfortable to say the least. It was similar to being in a cave with bats you cannot completely see, yet can hear all around you. When he tried to stand, although his legs still felt like anchors, they would shriek back and then forward again as if expecting a command. Sometimes he said boo just to be alone. Boo scattered them like dust. Only Carson spoke to him and mostly he was interested in knowing everything possible about the red barrette. He thought it gave him power, but then, people have always looked for a talisman, Ansley rationalized, remembering his rainbow family as well as Beatrice's braid. The power was in the believing.

His patience was wearing thin and time was not on his side. He had to meet Beatrice and the others tonight. A wicked idea hooked into him and ripped across his tolerance. He asked for Carson to visit. He wanted to show him the previous owner of the red barrette. Carson came obediently and Ansley drew Beatrice's braid from his breast pocket like a sword. They had never seen black hair. Ceremoniously he unwove one side and placed it like a crimped wig on his head. He stood tall and looming. Admittedly he must have been a horrendous sight. They screamed and ran stumbling over one another, demon, Ansley thought, was the verdict.

"Take me to the tree," Ansley boomed.

Carson immediately motioned for Ansley to follow and, like divers, they went deeper into the undergrowth. It was unbearably hot. Sometimes Ansley had to slither on his belly like a snake through the small openings. They seemed to wind around and around like tangled and intertwined burrows and he felt as if he were a fish weaving through mangroves, or as if he were navigating an intestinal track, and he tried not to think about the slime and excrement that lay festering in the heat. All around them were eyes, some were drawn on walls, some belonged to bodies. The roots snagged at him like barbed wire. He was obscenely big. The twists of corners were silvered by touch and sharp as elbows. Little stoves were attached to pipes that were long meandering chimneys and hot to touch. Woven hammocks hung in corners. Beads made of vines and then somehow dyed red and yellow, possibly from the mushrooms, were strung onto roots hanging from the ceiling. Soon he could tell that they were beginning to climb up. He felt the air move, not a breeze, but almost. He could smell green. The tunnels they traveled through were smooth, mercurial, and worn, as if traversed many times. Carson's feet were as small and fast as a rat's. All the while Ansley thought of the yellow daffodils Beatrice had painted on his wall, waiting for him in his new home like little faces of sun. Carson suddenly stopped.

"We are close. Listen," he said.

They stood perfectly still and listening. There was stomping overhead. As if something were galloping back and forth. There was snorting as well.

"That is the monster," Carson explained. "The god."

Ansley recognized the noise. What was it? Each snort acted like a magnet, pulling his memory through his incomprehensive mind until, with a spasm, it connected, clink. A stag. It sounded like a rutting stag.

"Is it a stag?" Ansley asked.

"It is a monster. But it has eyes like you. You are brothers." Carson said, as he pointed up to a hole close to the noise.

"The roots of your tree are more alive than others," he said. "Be careful." And he disappeared into the black tunnels like a momentary flash of a fallen star.

Ansley looked back at the hole. Did it just blink at him?

Yes. It blinked its guillotine blink and he felt himself a cadaver trying to rise out of a hot bog towards the sun's sharp edges of experimentation. What was he doing and why? The world would end with or without him. Hadn't it always? A breeze though the blade mouth ruffled Beatrice's hair and tickled his neck like a kiss. Alright then, for her. A twisted branch was hanging low above the mouth. With a scream he jumped through the mouth, grabbed the branch, and hoisted his knees towards his chest a mere moment before the guillotine clamped shut. I am a superhero, he thought to himself, and laughed out loud. It was the laugh of a crazy man.

He swung over to the side of the tree. If you could call it a tree, more a skyscraper with, it seemed, an appetite. There were long rubbery drips that hung all the way down the tree and it took Ansley a few seconds to realize they were tongues. He stumbled against one and the taste buds closed like touched sea anemones. He stared at it in fascination. The tree was magnificent. Deadly, but magnificent. Its bottom boughs dropped all the way to the ground like a skirt. Its middle boughs reached straight out in all directions as far as Ansley could see. Its top went beyond the clouds. Ansley could not see the other side of its trunk. Where each knotted bough twisted, a guillotine eye spangled at him. The leaves were sharp as scissors. The fruits hung from vein-colored stems like beating hearts. They only hung from the middle branches. That figures, moaned Ansley. There seemed the fragile barbarity of flesh against metal about the tree, as if it were at war.

A snot-spitted snort interrupted his thoughts and made his body freeze. He turned around. The stag stared at him, a hair's breadth away. It was like looking in the mirror. Very carefully, he took a step backwards.

He could feel the tree's tongue on his bare head. When he pulled it away one of the little anemone buds clung to his scalp like a leach. Horrified, he tried to pick it off. The stag saw his opportunity and struck. Ansley quickly grabbed one of the long branches and pulled it, like a shield, in front of him, so that one antler stabbed the branch and the other pierced a tongue on the tree. The tongue squealed and shriveled while a colorless gooey sap leaked from blackening pierce marks. The stag was furious. It had pinned Ansley between the branch and the tree, but whichever way it turned, it couldn't reach him. It ripped its antlers from the tree, backed up, and was leveling its attack. It charged full speed at Ansley screaming in fury, at the last minute Ansley ducked under the branch and jumped on the stag's back. It raged like a bull but Ansley hung on. He knew it was either himself or the stag that would die that day. The stag flapped him around like a wet rag. Beatrice's hair fell from his breast pocket. He couldn't be without it. He let go of his hold on the stag and dropped to the ground. He grabbed the hair and just as the stag was leaning down to pierce him, he threw the hair into its face. It blinded the stag for a moment and he missed stabbing Ansley's head and hit his leg instead.

The antler penetrated his thigh and broke off. Ansley screamed in pain. He maniacally grabbed the unbroken antler and used it to heave himself up out of the snake pit of vines. He took his forehead and bashed the stag in the chest. Still hanging onto the antler he flung himself into a seated position on the back of the stag. He took Beatrice's hair and tied it around the stag's eyes like a blindfold. The stag went suitably mad and thrashed. But Ansley held on. It was heading towards one of the guillotine eyes. It stepped inside and the sharp edge sliced its ankle off. Then it fell into a coiled nest of vines and whimpered. For a moment he felt sorry for the animal. Then he felt the searing pain in his leg. He looked down and saw that it was a clear cut. How was he going to get the antler out? Its rough edge was so sharp. He was worried that he might bleed to death if he removed it. He hopped on one leg towards the tree. How was he going to get the fruit down? He couldn't possibly climb the tree with his leg now. Also the thought of hanging onto a tongue like Tarzan filled him with disgust. He was going to have to knock it down. He picked up broken bits of vine and started throwing them at a particularly large piece of fruit. A few pieces stuck like marshmallows to a stick. The very fine hairs were like needles on the fruit. It was hopeless. He really needed something to wrap around the fruit stem so he could pull it off. Would a bit of tree tongue work? He didn't want to waste Beatrice's hair. He'd need her hair to tie around his leg when he had to walk out of here. And how was he going to retrieve her hair from the stag anyway? He couldn't thing about that obstacle. One thing at a time. He took a particularly sharp vine and cut off a piece of tongue the size of a rope. He knew how to tie a lasso. His country lessons had come to his aid more times than he could count in his life. The tongue wiggled like a snake coming to terms with its end. He let it shake the life out of itself. When it had finished it felt like slimy Silly Putty in his hands. He stretched it as far as he could and tied the lasso. It took three efforts before he finally hooked a fruit. When he pulled, the fruit stem severed, and out of its broken stick curdled a brown substance that seared right through the vines when it reached the ground. A good lesson to have witnessed, he thought.

He looked at the stag. It was rapidly losing blood. There was no way it was going to survive, poor creature, he thought, as he watched it licking its own blood in vain. Ansley couldn't just leave it to bleed to death. Very slowly, partially because of his leg, but also because of caution, he approached the stag with the fruit stem held between his thumb and forefinger like a vial of poison. Of course, it was a poison. The animal kicked and snorted manically when he approached. Ansley reached his hand towards the stag's head. It began to stop thrashing, it slowed and moaned gently. Ansley placed his hand on the stag's forehead. The animal just looked at him, breathing heavily and began to relax. It was as if he understood and he tipped his head back and opened his mouth. Ansley could have cradled him, such was the tenderness he felt, but he was in pain. They both were. He caressed the stag's jaw and then dropped the fruit stem down his throat. The stag immediately went limp in his hands.

Ansley closed his eyes and wept for both himself and the stag, for the love they wanted and the disappointed beast within themselves that their anger protected. It's true, like his father had said, all those years ago, they were brothers.

After a long while, he lifted himself up and had a good look at his leg. He'd probably lose it, but right now he needed to use it to get to the others. He took Beatrice's hair and tied one end to his wrist and the other to his thigh, just above the antler, and like a string puppet he lifted and lowered his leg. He wrapped the fruit carefully in a thick seed he had split open like a coconut, then wrapped a vine around it, which he tied into a loop and hung around his neck. There were still the same difficulties as before, still the heliflies, still the acidic mushrooms, only now he'd accomplished what he'd come to do and so had a greater amount of confidence. He looked around at the complex interfolds of root and tree. The air, like sandpaper against his lungs, there seemed no end to the jungle he was in.

Think of getting out and you will, he told himself. He thought of a river and how it soothes over the half-earthed rocks and bank roots extending as finger hooks, weightlessly molten and healing. That's how he would move through this forest. He thought of the moon's face hidden in the river's black surface, buffing along boulder and fallen log, and when he closed his eyes he saw his own face, pale as the moon and shimmering as it breaks apart and repairs itself again and again, like a trick. He flattens himself into a reflection only and floats down the river, through the forest, as soundless as blood through a vein. He didn't think. He didn't feel. He simply intuited movement.

He was alive. The sun had not completely set. He had the fruit. Those were the main things. He kept repeating them over and over like mantras. Until he finally reached the edge of the forest, and with one step, he was out. Was that true? Could he just leave as easily as he'd come? Transformed, yes of course, but could he just walk out and leave it behind as if stepping out of hell? We have choices, he thought to himself, and it gave him courage. He'd walked out of the city. He'd walked out of the phosforest. Where else would his legs take him? Or maybe he would die. He was losing quite a bit of blood. He looked behind him and saw his trail. A footstep, a wavy drag and drops of black blood. It reminded him of an aboriginal painting he'd seen in a museum. It was after he'd moved to London. He had been living in the warehouse then. The museums were completely unmanned as the doors had all been broken off. It was magical to view the paintings through spider webs in the steely dark. Ansley even thought of living in a museum but felt that he was too foul. He worried that the art might enter his dreams and his dreams were already invaded enough.

The river in him was beginning to wane and just when he needed it, a small thin trail of green smoke piped its distant signal and before him, a puddle of rain. He dipped his hands like goblets into the water and drank. The moon was huge. The water was black but tasted clear and bright. He cleaned his wound. But the antler was poisonous and his skin was beginning to foam and seal around the antler spike as if digesting it, embracing it. The pain was savage. It left him delirious. How could he go on? He looked towards the green smoke and saw that it was separating, becoming thinner and thinner, he was too late, he thought, it won't work anyway, I'll just lay down. He rest his head on the sand and closed his eyes. Give in. Give in, the world said, give up. And he could feel his breathing begin to slow, something crawling inside of his chest, as the poison entered his heart and made it, finally, finally, stop.

41

Nelly was there, smacking his face, wake up! Wake up! He opened his eyes. Somehow, he was underground, the sky was rock, fossils like constellations, lit up with glowing stalactites. Something was moving inside of Ansley's tongue, he gagged and spat a small beetle from his mouth. "Careful!" shouted Nelly, as she rushed to collect it, "that's Pupil," and she placed him inside a red-velvet-lined matchbox. "There you go baby," Nelly said, and placed the box in her pocket. She sat down next to Ansley. "I mean, I understand how important it was for him to spread his wings and everything, but it's good to have him back, you know?" she patted the matchbox, "now, what will we do with you?"

Ansley looked around. A clear river ran over red rock. Inside it there were shoals of lime green fish. A raft was in front of them and on the other side of the river was an endlessly long staircase that appeared to lead towards a small fleck of brilliant blue. Nelly saw him looking, "That's sky," she explained, "but it's eons away, and I don't mean eons as a figure of speech."

"Am I?" Ansley couldn't bring himself to say the word, he took a deep breath, "Am I dead?"

"Weeeeell, it's complicated," said Nelly, as she picked up a flat rock and skimmed it across the river. It skimmed to the other side in three equal bounces. "Did you see that?!" She punched her fist in the air. "In three!" and she held up three fingers to a man across the river and at the foot of the staircase.

He gave her the thumbs-up. "Nelly! Can you be serious for a minute?! What the hell?" said Ansley.

"No, no, no, not hell, don't be so dramatic. You're in between. So you're not dead per se but you're not alive either. You see, little Pupil here sucked up all the poison for you, so your heart started again, isn't he a star? Honestly, so, so generous, anyway, you were already here, in Charon's Land, because, you know, it takes a while. Paperwork and whatnot, plus, Pupil's only little with a small belly, a slow sucker."

"Is this a dream? I must be dreaming," Ansley pinched himself. It hurt. "Who is that?" he pointed towards the man in the long black tunic.

"Charon, aren't you listening?" said Nelly.

"The guy that gave you the thumbs-up is Charon?"

"Well, we have a particular relationship. I'm a regular visitor. I've know a lot of people that have found themselves here, mostly related to or as a result of artistic temperament, so … "

"So you skip rocks with Charon?"

"To be fair, there is not much else for him to do."

"How many of your friends have actually left?"

"Can you be more specific about what you mean by 'left'?"

"How do I get out of here?!!"

"You want to go back to Earth?"

"Yes!!"

"Are you sure?"

"What else would I want?"

"It's fun to be a ghost! Honestly, you'd love it, you'd hardly notice the difference, you wouldn't have to worry about the sunlight or any of that malarkey. Plus, I have this friend, Izzy, she's single, I have no idea why, she's not mutilated or decomposed or anything, I think you'd really like her."

"What?! NO! No, no, no, I just want to go back. Can't your friend take me back?"

"Okay, if you're sure that's what you want, I can't promise anything though, it might not work," she took out the coin she'd stolen from Dex. "See this," she flicked it in the air, "it's got your name on it."

"I have one of those! The Prophet Jude gave it to me!"

"You mean Jude's human casing?"

"Yes," said Ansley.

"Is that so? Keep it safe. And, if you ever meet the actual man Simorg, make sure you give it back to him," she said, and turned to Charon. "Ronnie, I've got something for you, send Fang over."

Ansley saw what looked like an eel twist its way through the river towards them. An Atlantic wolfish poked its head out of the water. It was hideous to look at, colorless with bulbous, cataracted eyes and four unsymmetrical fangs sticking out of its mouth.

"Hey, boy," said Nelly, as she bent down and pated his warty head, "give this to your daddy," she slipped the coin between Fang's teeth. Fang swam back to Charon who was waiting for him at the side of the river.

"I don't know about you, and please don't take this the wrong way, but there is a striking resemblance between you and Fang," said Nelly.

"Um, how could I not take that the wrong way?" said Ansley.

"Don't get snippy. I'm just saying that I could feel Fang feeling connected, you know? And, honestly, this whole 'brother from another mother' vibe could really work in your favor. Ronnie spoils that eel rotten, listens to every last thing Fang says and he's a talker."

"How will he know what the coin is?"

Nelly laughed, "oh, the living, they just crack me up! Trust me, he knows. Look, here he comes," she pointed to Fang making his way across the water. When he reached the bank, he sprang up, like a flying fish, towards Ansley and sunk his largest fang into the place where Ansley was told he had a third eye. "Thanks Ronnie," Ansley heard Nelly say, before everything went black and cold.

***

He was laying on the sand once more. The phosforest was behind him. Ahead, he could see the green smoke. He touched his forehead and the skin was smooth. Had that really happened? He inspected his leg and the infection seemed to have gone. It still hurt, the antler was still impaled in his leg, but it wasn't an angry, deadly pain. The pus had gone. He could make it. There was no time to think about Charon and Fang and Nelly, he just needed to move, so he stood up, and with the help of Beatrice's hair still tied around his thigh, began to shuffle forward. He concentrated on walking his string-puppet walk. One step at a time. He fixed his eyes on the green ribbon. Hung his heart on the green tail. He burned his path instead of walking it. The night sky slid over the horizon like frozen water, he slipped over it, growing colder, and with every step he gathered himself, blew into himself, and somehow kept the fire alive.

42

Pele Agnimitra walked to the edge of the sea. Blue globules of fire caused by leaking fracking wells organized themselves into stepping stones that led past the horizon. She leapt from blaze to blaze, her shadow as miasmic as oil in water, until she reached the boiling space above the vent that led to Jude's lair. A cherub sat on a raft shaped like a poo emoji. It was odd, but Pele Agnimitra kept her composure, "Tell Jude I have the girl," she said. The cherub rolled his eyes, flicked his cigarette into the water, dove beneath the waves, and slipped through the vent.

Jude was in his bedroom, resting, after swimming lengths. His exercise regime was definitely working as he could feel his digestive muscles were unquestionably tighter around his snack. He rang his little bell and a cherub arrived.

"Yes, sir?"

"Please remove the shoes of my last snack," he said, indicating a pair of trainers beside the hearth. "And light this fire. What use does a cherub have for shoes anyway?"

The bell cherub said nothing and looked away. Suspicious, thought Jude.

"You know something infidel! Speak!"

"They know that shoes give you indigestion, Sir, so they wear them in the hope that you won't eat them," the cherub said, and lit the kindling with a slow burning phosphorescent slime that resembled a fire.

Hum, thought Jude, I shouldn't be so transparent, "Very well," he said, "anything else or are you just sticking around for the joy of the risk?" he turned his snake head towards the cherub and flicked his tongue.

"The lookout says that a woman is here to see you," said the cherub.

"A woman? What kind of a woman?"

"The normal kind I think Sir, her name is Pele something I think," he said.

"Pele Agnimitra?! A fire sprite," he groaned. "The worst kind of woman, not in the beginning of course, in the beginning it's exciting, sparklers, fireworks, etc., but then, they just burn you up. What does she want?"

"She says she has the girl," said the cherub.

"The girl? THE girl?!?! Why didn't you say so in the first place you idiot!"

In ten minutes, Jude arrived at the surface wearing his going-out fedora. "Hello Pele," he slithered around her in a circle, careful of the blue fire, "it's been a long time. I don't normally keep beautiful women waiting but you caught me mid-digest." She increased the flames around her and Jude sprang up onto the poo emoji, "Get off," he pushed the cherub into the water. He didn't want Pele to know how desperately he wanted the girl, best to just be annoying, so she'd get straight to the point.

"And I don't normally fraternise with snakes," said Pele.

"You did once," said Jude, "I seem to remember an evening of fondue."

"Shut up Jude. I'm here on business," she said.

"Cheesy business?" Keep it cool, keep it cool, he kept saying to himself.

"You know what? Never mind, I'll go elsewhere," she turned around.

"Wait! I'm sorry! I'm sorry! I was trying to be funny, forgive me, my humor is lost on most," he said, "much like my charm."

"I can't argue there," she turned around.

"I have my flaws, what can I say?"

"And I have the girl, in moth form, enflamed," she showed him the candle. A blue pygmy moth was caught, unsinged, in the flicker. Jude coiled to take it. "Not so fast. You have to do something for me first," she said.

"Anything," he said.

"Give my sprites human form," she said. "I know you have human casings and I want them to house my people."

"Why? Isn't your wispy nature a part of your magnetism?"

She looked at him directly, held the flame under her eyes, "You don't know do you?"

"Know what?" he hated this kind of game.

"I hear that there will be a scattering soon. Fire sprites are elemental and we need form, human form, if we want to be a part of those that reorganize," she said. How had she known this and he, Jude the Great, hadn't? "Do we have an agreement?"

"How many casings do you need?"

"How many do you have?"

"Two hundred," he said.

"We will take three hundred," she said, knowing he was lying, "put them in a boat and bring them to the shore in one hour."

"Done," he said, and slipped away.

"And Jude?"

"Yes my sweltering lamb chop?"

"No cherubs."

"You don't make it easy, do you?" he said, and swam away.

No cherubs?! No cherubs?! That probably meant giving her his entire stock, he sulked, as he entered his house. Why oh why had he told her about his emergency casings? He was obviously trying to impress her with his forward thinking. He needed to learn how to keep his big mouth shut. He opened up his storage cupboard and gazed at all of his sleeping reserve bodies, just waiting for his digestion, stockpiled and numbered. Three hundred and fifty. At least he would have a few spare. Their little jars of DNA were resting on shelves above their heads. She hadn't asked for genetic coding and he wasn't giving freebies. So there.

He shouted for the cherubs and they came running. "Sir?"

"Put these jars with the others in my library. And take three hundred bodies and put them on the tugboat. Quickly! Quickly! We need to dock in fifty minutes!"

He needed to think. He went into his library, coiled up in his favorite arm chair, and watched his twinkling green helixes. A scattering eh?

43

Dex searched the tree for Marianne. He went outside and shouted her name. Ahead, he could see the pile of shimmering moths. He ran to the pile and started searching frantically for her form. Martin landed on his shoulder, he stood up and the bird nuzzled his chin with her small feathered head, then she shifted into a woman.

"She's not in there," Martin said.

"I know," said Dex. "She's been taken or killed and it's all my fault."

He put his head in his hands. What have I done? I should have been with her instead of brooding in jealousy, he thought.

Martin stood above the pile and blew her breath over the moth bodies. One by one they woke and circled her, flitting all around her hair and face, speaking to her with their delicate wings. The formed a giant candle with a blue pygmy in the flame.

"I see," she said, "fire sprites," she explained to Dex.

"Fire sprites?! How can we save her from fire sprites?"

"I don't think we'll need to. If I know Pele Agnimitra she's used Marianne as a bargaining tool and I can think of only one person she would want to make a deal with," she put her hand on Dex's back.

"Jude," he said, with his heart in his throat.

"Yes, go to Jude's lair and you will find Marianne," she said.

"But what if Marianne has already been killed?"

"It wouldn't be wise to kill her. Plus, Pele is not a murderer, she's a maverick, a trickster, knowing her, she'll probably have given Marianne a way out. The bigger question is what was Pele bargaining for?"

"I didn't think fire sprites wanted anything," Dex said.

"No, not on this planet, but … "

"But if she heard of the scattering."

"Yes, have you told anyone?"

Dex didn't answer. His shame ran deep. Martin stepped forward and placed her hand on his forehead and what she saw shocked her.

After Ansley left with the others, Dex had entered the room where Ansley had been sleeping. He sat on the bed, wondering what to do with his anger. Beatrice's paintings still covered the walls, but something had been added, a poem had been written beside a snowdrop. He knew it was Ansley's handwriting.

M,
I know
how things weather through us
and everyone cracks –
I pray
we can fill the gaps
with something
as starlit
as love.

Had she read it? Is that why she was risking her life to meet them? His rage shifted him into a fox and he ran from the room, the tree, his friends, and the possibility of a new planet, of anything good. He found himself on the hilltop once more, coin in mouth, the pub appeared and he entered.

The landlord was behind the bar pulling a pint. When he saw Dex, he threw back his head and laughed, "Women, eh? I didn't expect to see you so soon," he said, "trouble in paradise?"

Dex spat the coin on the countertop, "End it," he said, unable to bring himself to say Ansley. End Ansley, but that's what he meant.

The landlord picked up the coin and held it up to the light. "Now, I would, gladly, I really would, but there is one teeny, tiny problem, see, this coin is a fake," and he tossed it back on the counter. "I'll buy you a pint though?"

"A fake?! How can it be a fake?! It's the same coin that you gave me!"

"No, lad, it isn't. Look at it," he said.

Dex looked and saw that the coin was a regular two-pound piece.

"Seems to me someone did the old switcharoo, classic, that one. But listen, I like you, don't know why, but I'll tell ye what, I'll make it hard on the pale worm, I will. I don't know if death will answer, but I'll bring it knocking. Until you get me that coin, it's the very best that I can do. Don't worry, it just might do the trick."

Martin removed her hand from Dex's forehead and looked up at the moon wondering what to do, to say.

"I'm sorry," said Dex, "I just reacted, I'm so sorry."

"I can't say what the punishment for this will be, but I know there will be one, you will be challenged, here or elsewhere. My trust in you has waned," said Martin.

"I understand."

"But my love hasn't. There is still time for you to make this right. Fly to them. Help. Marianne loves the loyalty, the strength, in you. Remind her," she said.

"Thank you Martin. I'll leave now, I just hope I'm not too late," Dex hugged Martin and shifted into a falcon.

"We will offer you cover," Martin said, shifting also, and letting out a shrieking bird call. The hillside erupted, rose, and flocked over Dex as he flew towards the green smoke.

44

The tugboat full of Jude's emergency casings maneuvered into the bay where Pele and the fire sprites were waiting. Pele spoke to the enflamed Marianne, "The decisions I make are to secure my own people. Remember that, should we meet again. The flame will go out. Prepare yourself," and she walked forward to meet Jude.

"So, we meet twice in under twelve hours, aren't you a lucky woman?"

"Aren't I just," she rolled her eyes, "are they inside?"

"Of course," said Jude. "Unload the casings!" he called to the cherubs. Three hundred cherubs lifted three hundred bodies from the tugboat. It was a spectacular sight, the huffing, puffing cherubs and the bodies that hung from hangers like jumpsuits. "I guess you won't be needing the hangers," said Jude.

Pele nodded towards the waiting fire sprites and, en mass, they flew up the noses of the bodies, filled each form, as the cherubs landed them gently on the sand. One by one, the crowd began moving, like string puppets finding their legs and arms. The crowd walked around one another, disjointed, but slowly mastering each movement. Small clouds of smoke escaped from their mouths and ears and they walked around searching the eyes of one another. Their eyes had little dancing flames around the pupils, and when the fire sprites noticed other family members or friends, they whooped, hugged, and blew flaming rings into the air.

"Looks like my little secret stash was a real hit," said Jude. "Now, for your half of the deal." Pele gave him the candle, which he wrapped his tail around and snatched. Marianne saw a small flicker of fire blaze, the extinguisher, inside of Pele's gaze as she nodded towards the candle. Marianne understood that her flame would extinguish soon and that she needed to be alert. Thank you, she telepathed to Pele, who had joined the celebrations of her people.

"I just keep cropping up at the wrong time, don't I princess?" Jude flicked his tongue against the flame, it burnt. "Ouch, well, I'll figure out a way to get you out of here later, for now, my weaving beauties have come to the rescue." The spiders had made a special bubble to house the candle and keep it safe.

"Wait until you see my lair, you're going to love it, seriously, and little Emoli, you'll be amazed at how much he's grown," Jude carefully placed the burning candle inside the bubble and dove through the vent.

45

No boat, no car, no camel, nothing approached the horizon that seemed to run and run along itself searching for contact. Their eyes longed to connect with anything other than space and then suddenly a woman, skirts billowing and with babe in arms appeared to them like an anchor dropped on the sand.

"Who is that?" Valentine said.

"I think it's a mirage or something," said Oren.

"But we can all see her and look! There are others," said Beatrice.

"They've just sort of appeared."

It was true. They had appeared from the haze of the setting sun like refugees revealing themselves to a new land. The children held hands with other children. The women held babies. The men stared at their hands in longing. There was nothing for them to hold. The sight was troublesome and few were dressed in anything more than tattered shirts, none wore shoes, and each stopped when they saw the Growers. There were about fifty and they stood in a group a hundred meters away. Their bronze faces began to individually contour past the heat's vapours. They each wore the features of starvation. They stared at the Growers as if they knew.

"We can feed them," Beatrice said.

"There are too many Beatrice. We'll miss Ansley. I'm sorry but we can't just feed a few."

"We can make time."

"That's the one thing we can't make! Look at the sun,"

"We have at least an hour, hour and a half. Oren, we can feed these people!"

"I'm telling you, there is no time, besides they're doomed anyway."

"Then they'll die happy. Anyway, don't you dare speak to me about wasting time, Mr. Fire Eater. You owe me,"

"Owe you? I've apologized. I don't owe you anything. Valentine! Hey, Valentine, come back here!"

Oren ran after her but it was already too late. She was pulling food out of her stomach as if it were a Christmas hamper. The people were amazed. A few awkwardly stepped forward. A single woman stepped forward and accepted an orange. After that, Valentine was flooded with children. Beatrice stood next to her and started pulling food out of her stomach as well. Bananas, courgettes, corn, beans, if it could grow, they pulled it. Oren joined them and it was a bit of a feeding frenzy. When everyone had more food than they could carry the woman who had accepted the orange stepped forward and put her hand on Valentine's shoulder. Valentine put her hand on top of the woman's and then they hugged. The woman was crying. The tears traveled down her wrinkles like big silver boats down gorges. She smiled a toothless smile. Then everyone sat down to eat together. The woman motioned for Beatrice and the others to sit and join them.

"Thank you," Beatrice said, as she sat cross-legged on the dirt eating a runner bean.

Valentine joined her.

"We really don't have time for this," said Oren.

"Ten minutes is not going to make a difference. I don't remember the last time I sat down with a group of people and ate," Beatrice said.

"Nor me. This is fun," Valentine was smiling at another little girl. They both started to giggle.

"How about when we ate breakfast?" Oren said.

"I meant 'normal' people. Sit down Oren, seriously, just enjoy yourself and rest for a few minutes. Ansley will wait for us," Beatrice said.

"I'm not as sure about that as you are," Oren said.

They sat nodding and smiling at the people who were sharing what they had to eat with one another. When Beatrice finished she began unloading a little pile of food from her stomach onto the soil. She looked up and saw the green smoke.

"There it is," she said to Oren. "Ready for phase two? Valentine! Come on, we need to go," she called.

Valentine had been playing chase with the other children. She ran over to her.

"So soon?" Valentine said.

"Yep, see that smoke?" Beatrice pointed towards the smoke.

"Yes."

"That smoke is where we'll find Emoli. We need to save him and recover our pearl."

Beatrice went over to the lady and said goodbye. They hugged and shook hands. Then the lady clapped her hands together three times and immediately the whole tribe stood and began chanting. "Hyyyyeeeedaaaaabaaaa! Hyyyyeeeedaaaaabaaaa! Hoooleeeee! Hoooleeee! Hyyyyyeeeedaaaabaaaahoo!" Then there was complete silence as all eyes fastened on the Growers and waited. What were they meant to do? It was Valentine who bowed and caused the tribe to rupture into laughter and applause. Oren and Beatrice followed suit, bowing and waving until they could respectfully turn and walk away.

Again they began walking through the empty haze and again they felt their hearts pull like a song has the ability to pull one into another path, another life that might have been. They felt pulled from their bodies and rearranged into another version where they were stronger and better equipped for the task and they wanted it to be true. They wanted to be brave but knew that their same old fears waited in them like damp in a wall waits for the rain before it leaks. Each approached the horizon as an unwilling slave of himself.

Nobody wanted to speak of Ansley. Perhaps he didn't get the plasmid fruit? Or perhaps he got the fruit but wouldn't make it out of the phosforest in time? What would Beatrice do if he died? It was highly probable in the phosforest. Or better yet, what would she do if he lived? Oren was right, she had no business asking anything of Ansley as she was merely a Grower. Her body was merely a seedbed and she was bound by duty. But even so, did she care for him? Yes she respected his genius, but did she care for him like someone falling in love? She didn't know if she could be romantically attracted to him or not. Shame branded inside of her. She wasn't repelled by him exactly, it was just that she found him rather, well, fascinating. Fascinating in the way that hairless cats are fascinating because it just seems biologically wrong and unfair. She wanted to shelter him. So there was tenderness, but was it the type of tenderness that can become a romantic love? She didn't know. She needed more time with him and time was something she didn't have in spades. She took out his notebook and read another poem.

The Destroyer

We carry this injury
small as a bit of splinter
left behind
in our toughened skin.
It moves
around the body
piercing
so often
we no longer feel
how sharp
it dissolves into us:
patience,
it is sometimes called,
regret.

To spend more time with him would be exquisite. But she was about to explode.

"What are you doing?" asked Valentine.

"Reading and walking," said Beatrice.

"She is able to multitask our Beatrice," said Oren. "I wonder where Dex and Marianne are?"

Beatrice shrugged her shoulders and put the book away. She didn't want to share it with anyone. She wished she were alone. Oren always made light of things but she guessed he meant well. Before Valentine had the chance to ask Beatrice what she was reading she was distracted.

"Someone is coming," Valentine pointed her finger towards the expanse of green smoke.

His body, a tall spindly tree wavered against the day's purple beginning.

"There," Beatrice points, "Ansley."

"Looks like he made it," said Oren.

"Yes, but something is wrong," said Beatrice.

"He walks funny," says Valentine.

"He's hurt," says Oren.

"What is he using to carry his leg?"

"My hair."

"Ansley," Beatrice runs to him. "Ansley what happened?"

Her hair is knotted around his thigh like a rope encrusted with blood. His bare leg. She can see his veins blue as cracks in porcelain.

"Sit down," she helps him.

He breath is spitty and staggered. Hard.

"Here," he removes the vine from around his neck.

"I got it. The seed." His breath is labored.

"Thank you. But what happened? Here have a drink of water," she gave him a canteen and he gulped it down. After a while he caught his breath and began to explain. He told them about the phosforest and the stag, about the fight.

When he had finished, Oren put a hand on his shoulder.

"We'll get you out of here mate," Oren said. "I promise. Now, let's do this and be done with it. Are you ready to start? Do you have the energy?"

"I am and I do, but we should wait for Marianne and Dex," said Ansley.

"We need to start digging somewhere, I mean, we can't wait to find the point of entry. It could be anywhere, there is smoke all around us," said Beatrice.

"Good point. The haze of smoke seems to levitate above a section of ground about a mile long and wide," said Oren.

"So no place to dig," said Valentine.

"No obvious place," said Beatrice.

Then the sound of a small bell. A noise so soft and constant it could easily have gone unnoticed. How a goat's bell absorbs into a rural landscape. Beatrice searched the desert. It was like standing in the middle of an empty dinner plate. There was nothing but sand, sand and the green smoke that rose from some indefinable place. Rose is not the correct word.

It emanated.

Just as the woman with the flypaper hair suddenly emanated.

Her gummy grin, her eternal, encrusted skin like fossilized amber. There was life in her that shook persistently like the bell attached to the chain around her ankle. She took a dirty feather from her hair and placed it on the ground. She motioned for Beatrice to follow. Beatrice understood at once, she nodded, opened her backpack, took out the towel, and unrolled her collection on the sand.

The woman picked up two ends of the towel and flicked it into the air. The feathers scattered, a bird caught by a claw and the meat devoured, the feathers were many. The woman with the flypaper hair hummed and positioned the feathers into a large rectangle.

A door in the sand.

When finished, she motioned for Beatrice to step inside.

"Wait," said Ansley. "What about Dex and Marianne?"

"This might be our only chance, we have to take it," said Beatrice.

"Beatrice," said Ansley, "let me go."

"Never!" Beatrice jumped inside and the door's sand began to pour, to empty like a time capsule turned upside down. One by one the others jumped inside the opening and disappeared.

"There!" shouted Martin at Dex. He was speeding through the sky, towards the green smoke and the entry point. Ahead of him, the sand opened like a waterfall. He watched as his friends jumped from the edge and into a deep, swallowing current. Dex dived after them into the hole and, seconds later, it closed.

The woman with the flypaper hair placed her palms on the surface of the sand and it smoothed into an endless covering once more. Then, she stood and walked away. The martins hovered in the air, a bell ringing inside each of them, like a secret flower, a golden bee. "The end is near," said Martin, "blessed be," and the birds flew away to prepare themselves for the scattering.

46

Jude held the candle and watched Emoli floating in his bubble like a sac of embryonic fluid. It made the snake feel a little, well, familial.

The spiders' bubbles are supreme feats of natural engineering. Absolutely no fluid gets inside, there is only air, though Emoli often looks as though he's swimming, swimming in oxygen, and he looks happy. Jude can't help but envy Emoli his innocence.

It's not that he believes things could have been any different for him, mind you, a snake follows his heart. He follows it still. It is a dark path and he doesn't shrink away from who he is, nevertheless, innocence is something he can't remember having. It gives him pause.

His accomplishments have always been the result of another's fear and he has accomplished much. Yes, he has much to be proud of, but something occurred to him the other day while watching the spider feed Emoli. She liquidizes the food the cherubs bring, a water vole, an alligator leg, mangroves, and spits it out on a little leaf for him. And it occurred to Jude that Emoli was not afraid of her. He is not afraid. It confounds Jude, the boy is happy to see her even though the spider is twice his size. She treats him delicately. She is not kind or affectionate and yet, Jude feels she understands how important the boy is to her development. He watched this exchange from his deck chair, the two of them, coexisting like swamp twins, and it befalls him is that he is not the greatest evil. No. Evil for the sake of evil is not the greatest threat, for just as the sun and the moon share the same sky, good and evil will always live together. The greatest tragedy is when the world chooses to ignore him, to push him aside for their own benefit, and refuse the lessons he offers, in order to repeat them again and again. In reality, he's only ever wanted to be seen and his is a model of control that works. But, now, through this child's eyes, he is both seen, and, unfeared. Even, liked.

The truth is, he's grown fond of the child, despite conditioning himself otherwise and occasionally wanting to eat him. Jude can't remember ever being this content, it must be the child, and the child would want Marianne to live, but more than that, Marianne could teach the child all that Jude couldn't, human things. Perhaps Jude should just imprison her? Maybe killing her would be short-sighted, plus, without her, there would be no scattering. He doesn't want to scatter. He likes the home he's built and gave himself over to the thought of the three of them living in the lair he created like some abnormal family. A loathing spouse and a confined child, it had a certain sadistic ring to it. And, Marianne would never be able to resist caring for the child, who could with those cute cheeks?

He takes Marianne into the study and places the candle on his desk. Could it ever work between them? Or would she just break his heart like Eve? And, more importantly, could he really adjust to family life? He'd have to cut down on his hours. But, what would that actually mean? It was hard to say. Though he had time to think about it. He had Marianne and the seed, everything was going his way, he rang for a cherub.

"Pop the kettle on. An Earl Grey with extra bergamot will quench me nicely," he told the bell cherub. "And have you strained my cashew milk?"

"We can't locate the cloth strainer your majesty," the bell cherub replied.

"Confound it all to hell, do I have to do everything around here?!" Jude got up and slithered into the kitchen.

As soon as he was gone, the flame extinguished. Marianne took her chance and used the remaining strength she had to fly to the top of the bookcase and hide behind a jar full of green helixes.

47

When the pouring stopped they found themselves in water. Ansley suppressed a scream. A swamp festooned with heliflies, with heat. The air hissed with reptiles. The blood from Ansley's wound leaked a red snake through the dark water. Underneath mangroves flared, scaled nostrils. "Be quick!" he shouted, and they scampered to land, squatted above soil alive with larvae. Bugs. Everywhere Ansley looked he saw something crawling. The sound was a rhythmical scratch, an insect's sniggering. They hid behind large boulders of rock. It was still a cave. It was as if the swamp had been brought in or manufactured, like a theater set. Strange, because the setting didn't seem real, but the dangers were, this juxtaposition caught them off guard.

Ahead of them, a house sat on stilts like a fat bald bird. It was gray with abandon and wooden planks crisscrossed over its windows like stitches over a doll's eyes. It seemed full of pain and evil, beside it a water wheel churned like a large mechanical drum.

"That's the noise I kept hearing," Beatrice pointed to the drum.

The spokes were moving so fast they seemed to be one shape. The center was still and open like a black mouth. An army of heliflies swarmed the sky and entered the dark mouth, the hole. Cherubs were standing on the wide porch, smoking cigarettes and scowling.

Ansley gathered everyone together. He spoke in a soft whisper.

"That's where the cherubs live," said Ansley.

"And, it seems, the heliflies," said Oren.

"We need to enter," said Ansley.

"But we can't fly and I'm not going to swim," said Beatrice.

"There is no need," said Dex, who walked out from behind the rocks and stood before them. Everyone turned, trying to contain their excitement, all except Ansley.

"Dex! You made it! That's great! How did you get in here?" asked Oren.

Beatrice gave Dex a hug and introduced him to Valentine, who hid behind Beatrice's leg.

"Keep it down," shushed Ansley.

"Sorry," said Dex, "I was in falcon form when I saw the sand funneling and I flew through in the nick of time. Martin helped me," he said.

"And, Marianne?" Ansley asked, and Beatrice stiffened.

"Fire sprites," his voice was barely audible.

"How?" Beatrice and Oren looked at one another.

"Fire sprites," he said, "Martin knows Pele and thinks that most likely she took Marianne to bargain with Jude, which means she's probably already here," he said.

"Right, then we definitely need to get to the house," said Oren. "Dex can you fly us in or something?"

"Oh she's won't be in that house. That's just the staff quarters, she'll be in the mansion," said Dex, who had landed on the other end of the cave and in plain sight of Jude's antebellum manor.

"Mansion?" said Beatrice.

"Yep, follow me," and Dex lead the way.

48

Above them the trees were covered in a tangled Spanish moss as if draped in webbing.

"Look at all of those spider webs," whispered Valentine.

The stilts the house stood upon seemed to be knitted with spider webs, which gave them the appearance of being held up by a glistening cloud. They could see head-sized silken sacs dangling inside the enormous spider webs and thin threads, like motion lasers, attached from the central web to the surrounding trees.

"Trip wires," said Ansley.

"They are protecting Emoli," Beatrice said.

"And, possibly, Marianne," said Oren.

"How will we save them?" said Valentine.

"She's right," said Beatrice, "the webs are everywhere. We can't get close enough,"

"We could swim," said Oren.

"It's too dangerous, we'd be eaten," said Beatrice.

"I could fly you over one at a time, but I'm sure we'd be caught before I managed everyone," said Dex.

"Maybe, but what other choice is there? I can't see how we're getting out of here alive anyway," said Oren.

"Don't say that," said Beatrice, and she covered Valentine's ears.

"Look, there are fairies everywhere," said Valentine in a whisper.

It was true. Little green orbs bounced from everything as if they were fireflies. They noise they made crackled like an old movie reel or a just-lit match.

"Valentine, that's it!" said Ansley. "I have an idea. What are swamps made of?"

"Decay."

"That's right. And decay means gas. Maybe we could make a bomb or some fire? Valentine's little fairies would then actually become explosives. Hand me that stick."

Beatrice very slowly grabbed a long stick and gave it to Ansley. He poked it in the water.

"It's not long enough. I need it to reach all the way down to the bottom of the swamp bed. We need a long stick. I'm not sure how deep this swamp is. If you collect them I will tie them together. Move very slowly and silently. If we attract attention we are dead. I'm not sure how long we can remain unseen as it is," said Ansley.

"What's the plan?" said Dex.

"We'll blow him out of there," said Ansley.

"Great then what?" said Dex.

"I don't know. We'll react accordingly I guess."

"That doesn't sound like a solid plan. I don't like it," Dex said.

"Nor do I but, let's face it, we're not exactly on very solid ground here and if this works we might have an explosive," said Oren.

"We wouldn't have to do anything if I hadn't needed to waste our obsidian arrows on you," said Beatrice.

"Oh for goodness sake Beatrice, let it go will you?" said Oren.

"Beatrice!" yelled Valentine, as she cowered on the ground.

They all looked in the direction she was pointing. A spider the size of a cat was tiptoeing down the web wires like a trapeze artist. The hairs on its body glistened like black blades. Its jaw looked as sinister as a grinding machine. Ansley took the stick he was holding and swung. Thunk. He hit the spider square on the mouth and knocked it into the water. They each let out a breath. But the vibrations rippled up to the nest and suddenly hundreds of spiders popped out of the nest to look around.

"Quick a longer stick!" shouted Ansley.

Thousands of legs began to trickle down the web wires. They were caught.

Beatrice handed Ansley a fallen log. Together they shoved it through the water until it hit the bottom and large bubbles began to rise.

"Swamp gas! Give me a match," he shouted.

Oren unscrewed his waterproof container and gave him a packet of matches.

"Hurry Ansley! Hurry!"

Valentine hid behind Beatrice and began to cry. Ansley kept striking the match against the box. The sound of their legs moving was deafening. A thousand scissors snipping. The spiders were an arm's length away. Hurry Ansley! The match lit. The spiders were a breath away. Ansley threw the match towards the bubbles and boom! The spiders exploded, scattered like a plate of thrown black peas. The fire was bright blue with orange threads as if a star had fallen from the sky and landed burning in front of them. Then section by section the swamp began to blaze until it was a pool of fire. The serpents, the alligators, the insects left the water and started to invade the shore. Valentine's fairies caught fire and exploded like little fireworks in the air. One burst beside Valentine's head. She was shaking and too scared to move. Beatrice hurried over to her and picked her up. She held her next to a large tree.

"Climb up here Valentine and hide behind the Spanish moss, don't move! I have to go and collect Emoli. Oren is here with you. Do what he says and I promise I will come back for you."

"Wait Beatrice, don't leave!" Valentine scrambled down to follow Beatrice but an alligator approached the tree's base and hissed at her. She scurried up the branch and sat down.

"Please hurry!" she shouted after Beatrice.

Beatrice grabbed the fallen log, heaved it out of the swamp bed, and quickly pushed off the shore into the water. The tree was her float. She maneuvered around the burning torches like huge water lilies of fire.

"Beatrice what in the hell are you doing!" Ansley shouted.

But it was too late, she'd already disappeared.

"No!" Ansley jumped in the water after her.

His leg was seeping blood. And then suddenly a low rumble like a drill cutting through the earth made everyone freeze. Vultures flew down to the lowest branches. Heliflies in droves waited, suspended above the fires. The reptiles stopped moving. Nothing moved but the drill, crunching, biting. The fires cracked and popped. A rumble from the bottom of the earth burst through the water. Jude. A scaled and screaming bullet. Aghhhhhhhh! He soared through the sky and fell back in to the water like a boulder, his weight caused a violent tidal wave. In that wave, the tree that had been Beatrice's float, shot towards Ansley. She was not on it. It was as if a hammer had fragmented his heart.

"You!" he screamed, as he straddled the tree and began in vain to paddle towards Jude. "You killed her!"

Jude slowly turned around and faced Ansley. Ansley's body was the length of the serpent's snout.

"You dare to speak to me!?" Jude hissed.

"She was good and honest and you killed her!"

Jude thrust his neck up into the air and bellowed a great evil laugh. It was a laugh that shook the water like a storm. It shook the ground like an earthquake. It shook the moss from the trees. Valentine was exposed.

"Oooh and who do we have here?" hissed Jude, stretching his long neck towards Valentine.

"Touch her and I'll kill you!" screamed Ansley.

Again Jude laughed a laugh that thundered through the sky. Valentine fell from the tree.

"I like to have a bit of sport with my meat before I crush it," he hissed, and snaked through the water towards Valentine. She picked up a stone and threw it at him. It ricocheted off him like a grasshopper flicked off a giant's leg.

"Ha! The feisty taste the best!"

Suddenly Oren swung from a vine and jumped on Jude's back. Oren twisted and broke through his scales until he saw black flesh and then thrust the stick he'd been carrying like a sword into the flesh and began pounding it down like a stake in the ground.

"Aghhhh! Stupid fly! Get him!" Jude wreathed through the air like a snapping rope. The heliflies rained from the sky like torpedoes.

"Watch out!" Ansley shouted to Oren.

Oren ducked just in time but he heliflies kept coming, as if someone was spitting nails, and the serpent went on thrashing, like a live wire. Oren kept breaking off sticks, peeling back scales, and pounding the sticks into the serpent's flesh. Ansley jumped on to Jude's snout. Hung onto his eyelashes. Jude roared and the world was an egg that split.

Wait!

To Ansley's astonishment he saw someone inside Jude's eye.

A person standing there as if behind glass.

"Help," the person said. Without thinking Ansley reached down into his open wound and gripped the stuck antler and with a scream of agony he pulled it from his thigh. Blood poured like an unstopped cork. Ansley thrust the sharp antler into Jude's eye shattering it like glass. He stepped through the window.

"Quick follow me," the person said.

Ansley's leg was pouring blood.

"I don't have much time," Ansley said.

Together they slid and scrambled down the serpent's nasal passage. The person grabbed a thick handful of snot and thrust it into the hole in Ansley's leg. The bleeding subsided. The person grabbed a vein he'd attached to the serpent's uvula and with one strong arm around Ansley and another holding the rope vein, he abseiled down his throat and into his lung chamber. Jude roared with fury. His hot breath blew against them as if someone had opened an incinerator oven door. The person took an axe from his satchel and began chopping through the serpent's ribcage. Jude thrashed in agony.

"Hold on!" Ansley shouted to the person.

They each were grasping to a splinted bit of rib bone. He had nearly cut through the ribcage.

"Only one more to go," the person said, and crashed the axe against the remaining bit of bone.

It broke in two.

"Who are you?" said Ansley.

The person looked at Ansley. "Jude," he replied, and Ansley remembered what Nelly had said, but before he could recover the coin and give it to him, Jude shouted, "Finish it," and dived into the boiling juices of the serpent's stomach below.

"Wait!" cried Ansley, "this belongs to you!" and he threw the coin after Jude. It was the best he could do. Now, for the rest of it. Ansley looked around. He could see the serpent's heart beating in the corner like a frightened black bird. He entered the cage and walked up to it. He took the stag's antler and thrust it into the center. The puncture began to spurt like a firework. Ansley put the vaccine inside the puncture. Then he collapsed. Ready to die.

49

Considering the circumstances, it was remarkably easy. Beatrice rode the tree to the spiders' nest, broke off a small branch and made a hole. She peered through the hole and saw that it was empty. She'd have to get inside so with her fingers she made the hole big enough to climb through. It was like ripping cloth. She stepped through and looked around. It was as if she were standing inside a basket. It was completely silent.

At the bottom of the basket was a small pool of green water.

Beatrice knelt. The water was like a magnifying glass. Through it she saw another color. The color of flesh. She stuck her finger in the water. It tried to pull her finger through. She yanked her hand back. Then a large wave rocked the basket. Her foot fell in the pool and like a large wind tunnel it sucked her through. She landed next to a baby. The baby looked at her with golden eyes and lifted its chubby arms towards her. She scooped up Emoli and kissed him.

"What is this place?" she asked.

The baby nestled under her chin.

They were inside a big air bubble. A placenta inside the swamp. Beatrice could see snakes and alligators swimming frantically past. A forest of mangroves swayed and rocked in the huge waves. There was a great thrashing in the water and a large tail swiped them. The bubble broke from the web basket and began to float in the open swamp. The waters began to rise and the bubble bounced. Beatrice hung on to Emoli. She could see Oren and Valentine swimming and swimming.

"Keep swimming!" she called to them.

"Beatrice!" cried Valentine, as she grew smaller and smaller against the swelling tide. The serpent's body collapsed against the water like a missile. His pointed tail burst the placenta. Swamp water rushed into Beatrice's mouth. She clutched Emoli and swam with all her strength towards the surface light. Behind her swam Oren and Valentine. Where was Ansley? She looked frantically around. The three of them kept reaching and reaching towards the pale surface. It was miles away. But they kept going, kept trying. Then the second tide hit and knocked them unconscious. To see them was like watching pennies float down to the bottom of a well.

50

The sound surrounded her. A sonorous moan. A foghorn. A whale. Beatrice lay folded in its tail. Emoli was sound asleep beside her. She touched, disbelievingly, the fat rolls on his wrists. He was glowing like radium. The pearl was active and alive inside him. He was real. His protector was a whale. She touched the cool, wet, and slick skin of the whale.

It was real.

She felt her cheeks. Where she'd slept was rough and indented with barnacle patterns like beautiful pock marks.

She was real. She imagined the whales had dived deep and caught them like leaves on their backs. They rose to the surface. They breathed. She took a deep breath. Her lungs felt stiff with pain.

They were on the open sea. A family of humpback whales. Each whale carried a Grower. The wind was too fierce in their throats to talk, they each stood and frantically waved. They wiped the tears from their eyes. One was missing. Valentine. Also, she couldn't see Ansley.

Had he made it? She looked around and there he was, hiding in the shade.

"Ansley," she breathed.

Yes, just like pulling on a clean shirt, he thought, as he lay crouched by the tail. It was the only bit of shade he could find. He gave her a weak smile.

Her lips tasted of salt. Her eyes stung in the sun.

Of course, the sun! She saw that Ansley had been badly burnt.

With Emoli in her arms she very carefully scooted to Ansley and sat beside him.

"Are you hurt? How's your leg?"

She put her towel over his head and shoulders.

His eyes told her that he couldn't speak.

"Oh Ansley I'm so sorry," she said, and went to touch his cheek but he winced so she stopped.

"Of course, sorry," she said.

It was terrible. It was if acid were eating through his skin, sizzling, festering, bubbling, he was like an open sore.

She wondered if he'd make it. He was shivering. The blisters on his face were long and clustered like grubs, beside the pus, they seemed to squirm and weep.

Ansley had been the first to wake. The smell of himself woke him, which was ironic for a person without sweat glands. He could smell his skin burning. The smell reminded him of the vendors under London Bridge. Their signs simply read, "Meat." It didn't matter whose. He smelt of unknown meat. He looked down at his hands. They were red as beets, textured with blisters, and encased with secretion. His mouth was so dry. He rose, slowly, to a seated position and looked around. He was on the back of a moving whale. Life never ceased to surprise him. This would be a good way to die, he thought. The pain in him was complete. It owned him. He looked at his legs. There was no body left, just pain, just organs on the outside, bowels. I'm dying, he said to the innumerable glittering waves, and he tried to summon the strength to roll off the whale and in to the ocean.

But then he saw her.

"Crow." He struggled to pronounce the word. "Crow." His lips were indistinguishable from his face. The only features left were the holes: mouth, eyes, nostrils. "Heart," he said, "crow." She was there.

She was asleep with an infant he presumed was Emoli. The skin of the luminescent child reminded him of a jellyfish he'd read about long ago. They had made it.

Just then the whale lifted its tail. The drops of saltwater landed on him like searing bombs. With great care he slid towards the shadow the tail produced. Behind him he left a trail of skin. I am a snail, he thought, and sat against the barnacles that pierced his blisters like needles.

So this is the sun, he thought, and stared at it without blinking.

What did it matter now?

At first Beatrice thought they were sea spray.

Then the whales slowed down and a net of moths appeared in the sky. One landed on Emoli's cheek.

"Hello Marianne," Beatrice said.

Marianne flew to Beatrice's ear.

"You did it. I knew you would. Thank you, the moths can take you back now," she said.

"Thanks Marianne, but I'd like to stay here with Ansley."

"Ansley will be taken care of, I promise. He'll come with you," said Marianne.

A cloud of moths came and wrapped around Ansley like gauze. They lifted him into the sky and began to fly home. One by one, the moths cupped each of them and flew them into the air. Beatrice stuck her hand out and touched the mist. Beneath them, she could see a black hole in the ocean filling and swirling with water. The moth nets flew them back to the beech tree.

51

They all gathered inside the main room. All but Ansley, who had been taken to his bedroom. The opal flower centers were lit and glowing. Elsewhere illuminated moths hung in teardrop shapes from the ceiling or in lanterns beside doors and walkways. Two thick candles were lit on top of the table and between them was an open book.

Marianne fluttered around each of the Growers, kissing them with her delicate wings. She breathed in deeply the folds of Emoli's thick neck. It smelt like baby buttermilk despite the child being a little lit orb. The pearl, her pearl, she could feel it strumming into her. Its radiance entered her mind, her heart, and she felt peace. Then she changed into a woman and sat down beside them.

"The time is close," she said, "but first, I'm so sorry about Valentine. Did anyone see what happened to her?"

"I just saw her swimming towards the surface, before everything blacked out," said Beatrice.

"Same," said Oren, and Marianne nodded.

"Any word about Ansley?" Beatrice said.

"Yes. The moths have cloaked him in the webbing the corn spiders provided. It seems to have helped considerably. I think you could see him soon if you wanted," said Marianne.

"I'll go now," Beatrice said, and got up to leave.

"Wait, Beatrice. There is something else."

"What, is he dying?"

"No, well, actually yes, but in an alternate way. The moths found that a leaf cross had been tattooed on his stomach," said Marianne.

"What? Are you serious? Does this mean he can stand in for Valentine?" said Oren.

"Who knows? Strange things happen in nature all the time. Evolution. Things we can't explain," said Dex.

"But, yes," said Marianne, "I feel we should put him in Valentine's place," she took Dex's hand. She knew how hard it was for him. "I don't see that we have another choice. We need someone else, otherwise, we run the risk of not being able to scatter at all."

"What does this mean for Ansley? Will he evolve with us or just be a stand-in?" said Beatrice.

"That's precisely what we wanted to talk to you about. We can ask him if he wants to try, I mean, I don't see what his other options are to be honest, but it has to be his choice," said Dex. "We wondered if you would talk to him?"

"I'm sure he'd want to hear this from Marianne," said Beatrice.

"Actually," said Marianne, "he has been asking for you."

"Oh. What will we do if he isn't accepted?"

"That's what you need to talk to him about. We can't stop the process once it's started," said Dex.

"Meaning if he's not accepted he will just explode?"

"Yes."

52

Ansley had been sleeping for hours.

A poem burned in his brain like words written with a sparkler:

The Lucky Ones
Inside this churning. Pass
Happiness to one another
Where it seeds itself
And glows
Like coral.

He opened his eyes to spring. He was in the painted room. The seasons hummed around him. He felt his face. There was fine gauze around it and he could actually move his lips to speak. He could move his arms, his toes. "I am alive," he said.

She opened the door.

"Ansley," she said.

"Beatrice," he said.

"Can you believe we made it?"

"No, but I somehow knew we would." Speaking still hurt. He tried not to move his lips very much.

"How are you feeling?"

"Fine," he lied. "Is Emoli alright? What an amazing little guy."

"Oh yes, the little poppet, he's into everything and charming everyone."

"It helps his eyes are lit from the inside and he's otherworldly, like an angel or something, nothing like an angel to pull on the heart strings," Ansley said.

Beatrice sat down on the bed and held Ansley's gauze-covered hand. She could only see his eyes. They looked at one another for a long time. She touched his cheek. The cloth was warm and sticky.

"Ansley," she said. "Thank you for helping us. We would never have managed without you. You are the real hero here, not us, you. I wanted to say something. I'm no wordsmith like you are but, well, reading your notebook meant more, meant so much to me. I wish there was more time."

"Beatrice, I too … "

"Shhhh," she stopped him. "We sacrifice tonight."

"Sacrifice? Sacrifice what?"

"Ourselves Ansley. It's the scattering."

"What do you mean?"

"We are all soil in the end, you know, we were only ever hosts for these seeds. Emoli's glow is increasing and soon the Original Seed will activate."

"Do you mean I won't see you again?"

"That's what I wanted to speak to you about," said Beatrice.

"Scattering?"

"Living in a new way. You see the moths noticed that you were given the tattoo of a Grower. I know you're in a lot of pain Ansley but, if you could just move, just try, Marianne said there might be a chance that you could come with us."

"Where? What am I saying? Of course I'll go. I'll go anywhere."

"That's just it. I don't know. I've seen the world but I don't know what form we may take. But it may be that we are human or of human ilk. I'm not sure if you will dematerialize, I'm not sure if it will work, but you have the tattoo, which means you've been stimulated as a Grower so we should try. We could be together. We could have more time."

"I knew you were some crazy witch."

"You might even be able to feel the sun," she hesitated.

"It sounds like there is a catch."

"Yes. If it doesn't work you'll still explode."

"Seriously? Okay, that's quite a catch."

"There is not much of a life for you here, after we're gone. Also, we aren't sure what will remain, you know? Each species has its own story, so it's a risk for everyone, but compared to what we've been through … "

"Yes. You're right. Dematerialize me. Chop me to pieces. Stew me. Anything. Yes."

When she left, the room felt silent, that silence before something marvelous happens. Of course he would have agreed to anything. Sometimes when he listened to her speaking the syllables of her words reminded him of a stone skipping across a pool of still water. She made him calm in a way that Marianne never could. Beatrice just seemed to accept him, as he was, scabs and all. What could he grasp from this earth now but his own death? At least he had an opportunity.

He remembered being a child and finding a fox skull in the woods. He had placed it on a tree stump and watched a butterfly dip in and out of its eye sockets. Wasn't there some story about a butterfly fluttering around a skull and witnessing the entire world? He had always meant to look that up. Funny he didn't remember it until now, but could see it so clearly, life fluttering inside a dead mind, a dead idea, a snag of time. He himself was still formless to the shapes a life could take, yet it occurred to him that never again would a child find a skull in this exact spot in the woods. And life is purely our own unique experience of it. Duplication is improbable. And yet within all of our various experiences we share the same basic needs, the same emotions, each dreams, each mourns, each loves, each hates, each dies. What becomes of us if we do not record the truths that unite us? Why not believe everything and explode?

No one will know me, he remembered thinking, I will die and there will be no record of my existence unless, unless I enter a new world and expose it. That's what art is, entering change.

53

All his life, Ansley had dreamt of stepping into a world where there were no humans, only birds. Like that island that used to exist. It would always take him a while to realize that he was a bird as well. He would float on a warm ocean that rolled and fizzed along the sand. He would sway beneath mountains that rose out of the white water, sharp as new ideas. They were pockmarked with roosting places. At their bases grew trees taller than he'd ever seen, with trunks the thickness of houses. At dawn thousands of birds took flight, peeled, and folded over the sky like a fluttering gray muslin. He'd watch their shadow approach him on the water. This is the moment he'd fly. The wind would stir underneath his arms and he would notice they were wings. He'd open and lift.

The moths covered him as though he were a log they were feeding from. They covered and lifted him down the stairs as if he were on a stretcher.

"Leave me," he said, and they gently tore from his body, bits of his skin and webbing stuck to their wings.

His skin was so badly burnt that Beatrice could not tell that he was naked. The spider's web offered some coverage, but all the same, he looked like an unraveling webbed mummy.

There were huge blisters the size of dinner plates all over his body, like knots on a tree trunk, except the grooves, the folds were deep and crimson. Standing there with his arms held out to the side to keep skin from touching skin, he looked like a knotty and grotesque spruce.

"Here. Stand in Valentine's place," Marianne said.

Each Grower stood on a leaf emblazoned with their name. The leaves were magnificent carvings that burned with golden threads. Marianne stood at the table in front of the book, while Dex, standing in Emoli's leaf, held the child on his hip. This child was so radiant that it hurt Ansley's eyes to look at him.

"Before I read the incantation of the scattering, I just wanted to thank Ansley for his bravery. It truly astounds us and it is a great honor to accompany you on this journey," said Marianne, "whatever it may be. I have loved every minute of knowing you in this life," she said.

"Yes, it is truly a privilege to know you and we hope to see you all on the other side. All of you, I know we've had our differences Ansley, but I hope you make it through," Dex said, and turned to Marianne. "Now, before it's too late." Emoli was beginning to disappear into nothing but a bright light. The pearl was crowning and the new world was ready to seed.

"Yes," Marianne took the book and sang the incantation. "Hyyyyeeeedaaaaabaaaa! Hyyyyeeeeedaaaaabaaaa! Hooooleeeee! Hoooleeee! Hyyyyyeeeedaaaabaaaahoo!"

Oren and Beatrice looked at one another. It was the same chant the woman with the flypaper hair had used. It seemed a good sign.

"Well, here goes nothing," said Oren, and he took out his telescope.

"Let's hope it's more than that, let's hope we find one another again. Are you alright Ansley? Are you ready for this?" Beatrice said, as she, too, took out her telescope.

"As ready as ever," Ansley said.

"See you on the other side."

They each held up their telescopes. Ready? Everyone nodded and looked through at the pattern of dots. The telescopes began to glow and the top of the tree opened like the microscopic eye in an observation tower. The night's wide sky radiated down on them. A flock of birds hovered above the tree. The martins, thought Ansley. The dots inside each telescope mapped out a different constellation of stars that started swimming towards them like silver fish in a black sea. In starlit form, the spirit animals of the Growers entered the room and, with their long sparkling sinews, formed a circle around everyone. It began to spin. The child Emoli was the first to scatter. He rose from the circle, the tinkling of bells and laughter grew louder and louder, while beams of light surged through his skin until he was only a globe of brilliance. Around the globe, they all began spinning, all their dreams, their memories, their words, ideas, spilled from their ears and entered the starlit sinews, the globe, spinning. They orbited around the pearl and the sky twisted and clanked open. It was only a small hole but through it a bright white beam grew larger as it made its slow descent. An angel dropping, she hovered over the opening of the tree, then split like a prism and bore into the foreheads of Ansley and the Growers, still orbiting the pearl.

Their bodies became glass lanterns inside which their molecules, cells, seeds blew in tiny sand tornados. Ansley looked down and saw pieces of him swirling, dancing together inside the light, dust motes, he was becoming dust motes. The pearl traveled up the beam of light and Ansley felt bits of him wrenching towards its power. He turned to Beatrice. She was illuminated. The seeds in her crashed like hurricanes inside a transparent skin jar. Parts of her were already gone. The beam of light and the pearl had a magnetic force that lifted off pieces of each of them. Ansley watched bits of their bodies roll and bounce through the beam and up past the hole in the sky, where the pearl waited, beckoning like a bright sun.

A toe. A torn eyebrow. A nose and everything in it. His leg.

He turned once more to Beatrice.

Most of their bodies were gone,

sucked up towards the light.

She looked at him. His eyes are as beautiful and pink as a setting sun.

She smiled and her eyes detached

and floated away in the wind like green stones in a river's current.

He hoped for the chance to write that line – the wind in her eyes, green stones in a river's current – hoped he would make it somewhere and remember.

Their particles, their seeds stir up and hover for a moment like bees

Or a mob, or bats

before breaking free.

Scattering past, finger by finger by ear by thighbone caught

and sucked into the vacuum-black pinhole, large as

nothing is large

but the universe

when considered,

they burst into the air like confetti.

And there came the sound of bells, rejoicing.

He could feel himself fragmenting but there was no pain, no pain, nothing but his elements tearing away from him like chunks of star and igniting a burn that diminished back to zero. Red flares to black. Green flares to black. Purple, yellow. Zips in the air and words. In the end as in the beginning there were words. Letter tunnels. Attaching and reattaching to his lung, his spleen, his cheek, like lodestones. Everyone was gone, lifted, then snap. The sky shut. The other side closed around the pearl like a clamshell, inside it they floated, specks of dust, and a new world, landed on the hot tongue of possibility, dug down and began. Life. Again.